GONE GOAT

A Hidden Creek Farm Mystery
Cheryl K. Smith

karmadillo Press * Cheshire OR

I0689937

karmadillo Press
22705 Hwy 36
Cheshire OR 97419
USA
541 505-6440
www.karmadillo.com[1]
Copyright 2024 © Cheryl K. Smith
Author: Cheryl K. Smith
Cover Design: Zodiakk Books

---

1.   http://www.karmadillo.com

THIS IS A WORK OF FICTION.

Any similarities to people or places, living or dead, is purely coincidental.

Acknowledgements

To my Beta readers: Danielle Kimball-Smith, Jill Mahler, Debbie Smith, Terri Smith, and Jasmine Smith-Moore. I couldn't have done it without you.

Chapter 1

Pearl Kelly was excited about what she hoped would be a promising new direction in her goat raising journey. But almost before it began, things went wrong at her first show as President of the Middle Pass Goat Club.

She drove her Subaru Forester into the grassy meadow designated for the 4-H showmanship competition. She pulled in next to the vans and pickups with covers or cages parked under the trees nearby. The sounds of car engines and goat cries filled the air as a line of vehicles continued to maneuver into parking spots.

The competition was being held in conjunction with the Skunk Cabbage Festival, an annual event in Middle Pass Park every March during spring vacation.

Towering fir trees and the occasional maple bounded the park on two sides. Across from the show area were vendor booths, stages, rides, and other festival displays, with a large, colorful Ferris wheel towering behind everything.

Dressed in navy blue cotton slacks and a crisp mint green blouse, Pearl got out of the car with a large tan leather bag slung over her shoulder and headed for the show ring and judge's table to the left of the parking area. A clutch of women stood in front of the table that had been arranged for the judge and scorekeeper, while kids fidgeted and climbed on the temporary fold-out bleachers that had been prepared for the audience.

Her lip curled when she sighted Zora Vega holding court with a few women between the table and the show ring. She and the pudgy woman with rat-brown hair were like oil and water. Pearl had no tolerance for Zora's know-it-all manner but found it impossible to avoid her now that she was involved with the goat club.

Sarah, Pearl's friend and mentor, sat on a green lawn chair behind a fold-out table next to a teenager Pearl didn't recognize. They were focused on the contents of a thin plastic binder. A heavyset man with pomaded black hair sat next to them, drumming the table with his fingers while he stared ahead.

"Is the judge here yet?" Pearl asked Sarah, as she approached the table. Women in the group with Zora waved when she passed by. Pearl smiled and waved back before turning her attention to Sarah.

"Oh, yes. He's right here. This is Len Brubaker, from the Seattle area." She held her hand out in the direction of the man at the table. He stood and grasped her hand in a firm handshake.

"Pearl Kelly," she said. "I'm the President of the Middle Pass Goat Club. I'm so glad that you generously came to judge for us. I have your contract here in my notebook. We've agreed to pay you $100, travel expenses, and lunch at the festival. Does that sound right?" She pulled a notebook from her large purse and rifled through it in an attempt to find the contract she had prepared.

"Pearl." Sarah smiled. "Take my chair. I need to get up anyway." She stood and walked toward a group of women sitting on the bottom row of the bleachers.

Pearl went around the table and plopped into the chair next to Len. She bit her lip and continued to dig through her purse.

"Ah, here it is!" She turned to Len. "Our treasurer, Jenny, will give you a check at the end of the competition."

She placed two copies of the contract on the table, signed for the club, and passed them over to him for his signature. He signed, folded one and put it in his pocket, and handed the other one to Pearl. They shook hands.

The parking area gradually filled. Pearl went to find Sarah when a rotund woman with pale skin caught her eye. The woman, wearing worn flip flops, long shorts, and a red, flowered blouse, lurched through the crowd. She carried a large handbag that matched her blouse. The woman moved from person to person, talking to each of them until they frowned and moved away or checked their cell phone.

Pearl saw Sarah getting up from the bleachers. Before she could make a move toward her, the disheveled woman planted herself in Pearl's path.

"Why aren't the goats in pens?" she asked.

"We don't have the space. This is called a 'truck show.'" Pearl eyed the woman warily. *Where is this going?*

"What do the winners get?"

"Ribbons," said Pearl. She looked around for someone to rescue her. Sarah, deep in discussion with Len, didn't notice.

"How much do these goats cost?" The woman moved closer to Pearl. The odor of halitosis hit her like a sledgehammer.

Pearl took a step back, her patience wearing thin. "The cost varies depending on the type of goat." A teenager next to Sarah smirked and averted her gaze when Pearl caught her eye.

"Are these goats pets? I used to raise prize-winning goats, but now I only have them as pets. Do you know if any of these are for sale?"

"I don't think any of these children are selling their goats right now. Listen, I have to get ready to make the announcements." Pearl turned and walked around the table while giving Sarah an exasperated look.

The woman in the red blouse meandered through the middle of the show ring. She ducked under the rope near the metal bleachers. Pearl pulled a canary yellow paper out of her purse: the announcement sheet she had printed before leaving home. It had taken her more than 50 years to figure out that using different colored paper would help her to be more organized, something she didn't always succeed at.

When she scanned the area again, she saw the annoying woman heading away from the show as she made her way between the parked vehicles.

Chapter 2

Pearl checked her watch. Ten more minutes. Kids dressed in their show whites approached the table looking for the attendance sheet. Families and other interested people continued to fill the bleachers.

She pored over her notes, nervous about speaking. Before she could walk back to the judge's table, Zora approached with two dark-haired teenage boys in tow. "Pearl, these are my kids, Zander and Zeus. They both show championship animals. Boys, this is Pearl Kelly. Pearl is the goat club president." Chin out, she radiated superiority.

"Nice to meet you," said Pearl. She surveyed the two kids, a stick-thin boy in a black t-shirt, jeans, and a dark hoody with greasy strands of dark hair hanging out of it, and a heavier, chestnut-haired, baby-faced boy wearing the required show-white pants and shirt.

"Are you showing goats today?" she asked Zander.

"Yes, ma'am," said Zander, the boy in whites. "I'm 16, so I'm in the Seniors class."

"I'm raising a pig." Zeus sneered, staring at her with steel-blue eyes. "I don't like goats."

Pearl ignored him. "Well, good luck, Zander. I need to get ready to start the show."

She anxiously checked her watch. "It was nice to meet you boys. I'll talk to you later, Zora."

Zora nodded, and she and the boys walked toward the bleachers. Pearl watched Zora and Zander sit in the front row, while Zeus continued past them to a thin girl, also dressed in black, who stood near the parked vehicles. The two of them walked a few steps, stopped, and talked before looking around. They ambled to a nearby blue van and Zeus leaned into it, hands on each side of his head and nose pressed against the window. Pearl bit the inside of her lip, suspicious.

She turned her gaze to Zora and Zander sitting on the bleachers. Zora was in conversation with a gray-haired woman in overalls who sat next to her. Zander had turned to watch his brother and the girl. The two spoke to each other again, looked over at Zander, and gave him a thumbs-up sign. Zander swung back around when Zora said something to him.

Pearl scanned the field where the vehicles were parked. Zeus had disappeared, but the girl peered into the canopy of a white Chevy pickup parked farther from the ring.

Pearl looked at her watch again and shifted her eyes to the judge's table. It was time to get the show started.

"Sarah, are we ready to go? It's 10:00. I need the microphone. I'm going to announce that this is the showmanship competition, note the order of showing—beginning with youngest first, introduce the judge, and turn it over to him. Does that sound good?" Pearl's hand shook a little. She hadn't spoken to a crowd for a few years.

"Great!" said Sarah, smiling. "You'll do fine."

Pearl made her announcements, handed the mike to Len Brubaker, and took a seat next to Sarah. The youngest children—the Cloverbuds—had already retrieved their goats from their vehicles and stood outside of the showing area in anticipation.

"Bring your goats in and line up facing this direction," said the judge. One little six-year-old girl, adorable in show whites, walked her goat into the ring. Her goat, almost as big as her, was mostly well-behaved. The rest of the kids were seven or eight years old, and you could tell that they had been practicing with their goats.

Everyone in the bleachers seemed to be getting a kick out of watching them walk and pose their goats. Each child had a Nigerian Dwarf, Pygmy, or mini, unclipped because of the still-cool weather.

The goats were different ages and sizes. The two littlest ones, only a month or two old, were harder for the children to control. They flipped around, stopped to pee, or refused to move. The 4-H leader or the children's parents had coached them to answer the questions asked by the judge, such as the goat's breed or how long a pregnancy lasts.

As the judge determined placings for the Cloverbuds, Pearl noticed a lot of foot traffic between the show arena and the vehicles, as children, and some parents, got goats for the Juniors' showing. She spotted both of Zora's sons now sitting on the bleachers next to their mother. The girl had vanished.

By the time the Cloverbuds got their ribbons and exited the show area, the three Juniors were in line and ready to go. When the judge announced that they should enter the arena, they filed in and lined up with their goats. It appeared that each of them had raised a goat before because they were able to better control them. The showing went off without a hitch, and the judge asked questions to test their knowledge of goats.

The Intermediates were retrieving their goats from the vehicles for their turn in the ring. Pearl saw Zora sitting in the stands eyeing the vehicles as Zander came alongside the ring with his goat.

A loud scream rang out from the vehicle area.

Chapter 3

"**D**aisy is gone!" Sierra Lang ran wailing toward the bleachers. "Mom!"

Lindy Lang clambered down from the bleachers and ran to meet Sierra by the vehicles. "What do you mean she's gone?"

"Daisy's not in the van! I opened the door to get her and she was gone. Someone stole her!" She broke down again, as children and their parents rushed toward the parking area to check on their goats. The Intermediates, who stood by the ring with their goats ready, turned to watch. The judge announced the placements for Juniors and ended the show.

Pearl stepped into the ring and took the microphone from the judge. She made sure it was switched off and spoke to Len Brubaker. "Will it inconvenience you too much to take a half hour break?"

"Of course it won't," he said. "We're ahead of schedule because things went so smoothly till now. What a shame. I feel sorry for that poor little girl."

"Thank you for being so understanding. You can wait here or get something to eat." Pearl was grateful he didn't make a fuss.

She switched on the microphone and spoke into it. "Please try to remain calm, everyone. We're going to take a half hour break while we look for Sierra's goat. If you have an animal ready to go, you can sit and wait for the show to begin again or put your goat back in your vehicle. Those with animals still in their vehicles, please go check to make sure your goats are there. Be back here in a half hour to re-start the show with the Intermediates. We'll get a description of the goat and share it with everyone in a few minutes. Hopefully by the time we get back we'll have found Daisy."

Chaos ensued as a few of the men jogged toward the woods behind the parking area to see if anyone had gone there with the goat, while other parents fanned out to the exits to see if they could spot anyone carrying a goat. Some sat in the bleachers, with shocked expressions on their faces. Zora, looking unfazed, sat on the bottom of the bleachers next to Zander, who held his goat by the collar. Zeus had again vanished.

Pearl walked over to the now-hysterical Sierra and Lindy. "Can you give me a description of the goat so everyone knows what to look for? I'll notify festival management and ask that the attendants at the exit inspect vehicles as they leave so we can make sure that Daisy doesn't go home with the wrong person."

"She's a three-month-old Nigerian Dwarf doe. She has distinct markings, white with one large black spot on each side, black above the top lip, and a black tail. Sierra got her two weeks ago and had worked so hard on her showmanship," Lindy said. She hugged her crying daughter. "Ours is the maroon Toyota truck with the matching canopy. We backed in so it would be cooler for Daisy in the shade until it was time for the show."

"Is she microchipped or tattooed?"

"Microchipped." Sierra sobbed.

"Thanks, Honey," said Pearl. "We'll do everything we can to find her."

Pearl chewed on her bottom lip as she walked back to the table where Sarah sat. She picked up the microphone again. "Everyone, I need your attention. The missing goat is a Nigerian Dwarf doeling, three months old, named Daisy. She's white with black spots, in particular, the tail, above the lip, and one large spot on each side. If you see anyone with this goat, do *not* try to stop them, but contact a security officer to help you. You can find them throughout the festival grounds."

She set the microphone on the table and turned to Sarah. "I'm going to walk through the grounds to try to find her. We need to leave no stone unturned."

"Okay. I'm going to stay here with Sierra in case anything turns up. There's no sense in everyone going out."

Pearl walked through the food section, with booths that advertised standard fair food: cotton candy, hot dogs, caramel corn, ice cream, beer, hamburgers, fried dill pickles. The smells were inviting but she focused on the task at hand.

She wandered over to the building that housed the photography contest and themed vendors and nonprofits, but saw nothing out of the ordinary.

She traversed the aisles with booths promoting political parties, dog rescues, health care providers, and other nonprofit organizations. No luck.

In the themed section, she passed tables with medicinal concoctions made from Skunk Cabbage, ceramic Skunk Cabbage flowers, photos, and other art featuring the yellow-flowered plants, and even food made from the Skunk Cabbage plant for those who were more adventurous. Along with the themed items were all variety of slug representations—another part of the quirky festival. Slugs loved to eat skunk cabbage, so they were plentiful in its habitat.

Pearl paused to admire a photo of a beautiful banana slug perched on and eating a large skunk cabbage leaf. A tiny AI-generated Nigerian Dwarf goat wearing a purple cowgirl hat was standing on the slug. The super-saturated colors were stunning. *That would be perfect on the bookcase.* She checked the price and grabbed one of the artist's cards.

"Stay focused," Pearl told herself.

She went out and past the stage where a hypnotist spoke to five people sitting in chairs on the stage while the audience watched. Next to it a petting zoo held a variety of farm animals. The sign erected in front of the enclosure advertised free entry and alfalfa pellets for a quarter, which visitors could feed to the animals.

Pearl headed that direction. A long line stretched into the dirt path, with impatient children and their families waiting for others to leave the zoo to make room for them.

Pearl scanned the people in the area, and walked to the side of the peanut booth. The woman cashier had a face hidden under a mask of cosmetics, an incongruous choice for the job of peanut-selling. Pearl scoffed.

"I'm not going in," Pearl said to the woman. "I'm from the goat show and someone stole a girl's goat. Were any new goats brought in while you were working?"

"Of course not!" she said. "This is a reputable operation. If you have a problem, talk to Mr. Broadsky." She pointed toward the back of the enclosure to a man with dark, gelled hair.

Pearl put her hands on her hips. "I was just asking. Wouldn't you want every possibility considered if it were your goat?" She couldn't believe some of the people who work with the public, but she didn't have time to argue.

She walked around the petting zoo, stopping at each side to scan every animal. No Daisy.

She continued toward the trim, dark-haired young man. "Mr. Broadsky?"

He put on an artificial smile, showing bright white teeth, as he walked toward her. His steel blue eyes were piercing. "Call me Jeff. And who do I have the pleasure of meeting?" He held out a soft, uncalloused hand, that looked as though he'd never done a day's work.

She reached out and shook his hand. He had the grip of a dead fish. "I'm Pearl Kelly, president of the Middle Pass Goat Club. We're holding a showmanship contest for the 4-Hers and someone stole one of the goats from a vehicle before she could be shown. You have goats here, it seemed logical to check, just in case. But I don't see her."

"Of course you don't. We already have goats, so no one here needs to steal them. I'm sorry I can't help you." He clenched his jaw.

Pearl stepped back and swallowed hard. "I'm sorry, too." She fished in her pocket and pulled out one of the new Middle Pass Goat Club cards she had had made. "If you see a black-and-white Nigerian doeling, about three months old, please give me a call."

Jeff snorted, but caught himself. "Do you know how many black-and-white Nigerian Dwarfs there are in Oregon?" he said in a condescending voice.

Pearl pressed her lips into a thin line. She tried to relax her clenched fists as she sized him up. He couldn't be much over 20 years old.

He reached out and touched her arm. "I didn't mean to offend you."

Pearl recoiled. Her face turned red. "I'm just distressed by the theft. It ruined our goat show. I'd better get back now."

"I'll keep an eye out," said Jeff. "I'd like to help in any way I can."

Pearl bristled as she walked away. She could tell disingenuousness when she saw it. Her shoulders were slumped as she returned to the show area. Other searchers straggled in over the next 15 minutes with grim faces. No one had found Daisy, and Sierra sobbed, inconsolable. Sarah and Pearl agreed that the competition had to go on for the sake of the other exhibitors.

Chapter 4

"I have an idea," Pearl said to Sarah. "What if we ask Sierra if she wants to show someone else's goat? That way she has a chance to compete for the showmanship award, despite the fact that Daisy is missing." said Pearl.

"I think it's worth asking," said Sarah.

Pearl made her proposition to Lindy and Sierra. "I know you're heartbroken about Daisy, but I wanted to give you a chance to compete in the show, anyway. There's no need to have two losses in the same day. How would you feel about me asking one of the other kids if they would let you use their goat? Or, do you have a friend in a different category who might lend you a goat?"

Sierra gazed at her mother. Lindy nodded. "I think you should do it, Sierra. You practiced your showmanship so much," Lindy said.

"Okay," said Sierra, standing straighter. "I'll ask Jenny if I can use her wether, Diamond."

Pearl put her hand on Sierra's shoulder. "Sierra, I promise to do everything I can to find your goat. We don't have to give up just because we couldn't find her today."

Sierra held back tears and managed to squeak out, "Thank you."

AFTER THE SHOWMANSHIP competition was over, Pearl scanned the bleachers. Zora and Zander were preparing to leave. Still no Zeus. Pearl wanted to talk to them before they went back to their vehicle.

"Hey, Zora, Zander!" Pearl yelled as she strode across the ring. Zander startled and froze. Zora turned around. Pearl caught up with them.

"Congratulations on your ribbon, Zander." The tension went out of his shoulders and he smiled.

"Thank you, Mrs. Kelly."

She turned to face Zora. "Did you see that large woman in the red blouse going from person to person asking questions?" Zora had been raised in the area and knew most everyone.

"I think so. Was it before the show started?"

"Yes," said Pearl. "I also noticed her heading toward the parking area afterwards. Do you know who she is?"

"Oh, that's Annie Spink," said Zora.

"I take it she doesn't have goats," said Pearl. "She had some strange questions."

"She lives on the east side of town on a couple of acres. She does have goats. In fact, a few years ago I gave her a pygmy wether that I couldn't find a buyer for. I didn't want to bother taking him to the auction. Annie has a menagerie of misfit animals that she got from people who don't want them." Zora looked quizzical. "Why are you asking about her?"

"She acted strange and disappeared before Sierra discovered that her goat was gone." Pearl crossed her arms. "It was probably a coincidence.

Zora took a step toward the parking lot.

"One more thing, Zora. What happened to Zeus and his friend?"

Zora flinched and surveyed the area. "I'm not sure. He drove his own truck here, so they must have went home or to her house."

"Yeah, he loves his precious truck. He thinks he's too good to ride with anyone else," muttered Zander, sneering.

Pearl glanced at Zander, surprised at his obvious disdain for his brother.

Zora swatted his arm and hissed, "You're jealous because you failed the driver's license test."

His shoulders slumped and he dropped his head.

Pearl turned to Zora. "I didn't see him leave. When did he go?"

"Uh, I don't remember," said Zora. "Maybe when the Cloverbuds finished? I think he went home. Remember, he doesn't like goats. He surprised me even coming for part of the show. C'mon, Zanny. We need to get home."

Pearl clenched her jaw. She opened her mouth to say something, but thought better of it. "Okay, thanks. Have a nice evening."

Zora steered Zander by the shoulder as he trudged to their truck. Pearl watched them drive away. Zander turned and peered out the window at her until they got too far away to see.

Chapter 5

After she let her white Pomeranian, Buckley, out the door, Pearl collapsed on the couch. She rubbed her eyes, feeling as if she'd had a bad dream. Her first official act had ended in disaster. Despite club members, parents, and festival staff scouring the grounds, they had had no luck finding Daisy. No one reported seeing a person with a 20-pound goat kid leaving the park, either, despite a festival-wide announcement. Some 4-H parents had checked the other vehicles, with no luck. She wasn't in the petting zoo, either.

After a discussion with Sarah and Jenny, the club secretary, Pearl had agreed to call the sheriff's office and report the theft that day. Not that she expected them to do anything.

Another fear hit her. *Are all my goats in the barn?* The festival would be a perfect time for someone to burglarize houses—or farms.

She jumped up and rushed out the front door and to the barn to count her goats. Buckley caught up and followed her. Pearl's hands shook and she felt her blood pressure rising when she couldn't find two of the youngest kids. She frantically searched the barn, while she vacillated between telling herself that she would find them and believing that someone had stolen them. Buckley stood outside the loafing area and watched her growing agitation.

After 15 minutes of ricocheting around the barn in a panic, she found the little kids curled under the wooden sleeping bench, fast asleep and oblivious to her terror. Pearl picked them up one at a time and hugged them to her chest, while she gave a sigh of relief and willed her heart to slow down before she returned to the house.

Westin came out of his shed blinking when she walked back to the house with Buckley at her heels. He wore sweatpants and a white T-shirt, his face was covered in stubble, and his hair stood on end.

Westin had been Pearl's farm helper since her former farmhand Pat died the prior autumn. The quiet, dark-haired man in his late 30s had been at loose ends, so with a little prodding he had agreed to stay in the heated shed on the property through the winter, instead of the van he had been living in. Pearl couldn't believe her good luck having him there helping. She hoped he would stay.

"Are you okay? You look like you saw a ghost," he said.

"No, just a minor panic. I couldn't find the two youngest kids and freaked out. You'll understand when I tell you what happened at the showmanship competition." She closed her eyes and let out a sigh.

"I guess everyone was safe with you here," she said.

"Of course. But it must have been pretty bad for you to panic like that. Tell me what happened," said Westin. Buckley jumped at his shins in excitement until Westin bent down to pick him up.

"In the middle of the show, someone stole a Nigerian Dwarf doeling from a teenage girl there. Everyone kept their animals in their vehicles until their turn to show. When Sierra went to their truck, her goat was nowhere to be found." Pearl could feel her pulse hammering again as she talked about it.

"We searched the entire festival grounds with no luck. No one had seen anyone take the goat or leave the grounds with her."

"Wow," said Westin, at a loss for words. "What's gonna happen?"

"Well, first I'm going to call the sheriff to make a report of the theft. Then I have some ideas for tracking down the culprit, and some ideas about who it might be. The most likely scenario is that he ran into the woods behind the parking area with her. He would either have to be strong enough to carry her or would have a leash or something to lead her with. I don't see how a three-month-old Nigerian Dwarf could be taken out through the exit without being seen." Pearl chewed on her bottom lip.

"Let me know if I can do anything to help you. I'll keep my ears open while I'm in town. What did the goat look like besides being a Nigerian?" Buckley squirmed until Westin put him on the ground.

"She weighs about 20 pounds, white with a black tail, black mustache in the upper lip and one large black spot on each side. She won't be hard to miss because of her distinctive markings."

"Okay, Pearl. I'll help in any way I can. It's a bummer that this happened. It must have spoiled the goat show."

She wrapped her arms around her body. "Thanks. It didn't go the way I hoped my first goat show would. This is a lousy start to my first year as president of the goat club. We'd already done two classes when she went missing. Sierra borrowed a wether from a friend, so at least she got to compete in showmanship. She came in second place, too." Pearl put her right hand on her heart.

"You know, there *is* something you can do to help. I want to go to the Eugene Livestock Auction on Saturday for the next few weeks to see if anyone tries to sell the goat. Will you come with me this Saturday?"

"Sure. I'd be happy to go. I've never been to an auction before, so it should be interesting. And remember: I'm almost always here, so no one will get into the barn to steal a goat without me knowing. Try not to worry."

Chapter 6

Pearl sat on the couch, clutching Buckley and thinking about how upset she would be if someone stole one of her goats. She knew Westin was right. She had to let go of the thought or drive herself crazy.

After a cup of chamomile tea, she called the sheriff's office and spoke to Sheriff Dan Springer. She had expected to get a deputy, so when they put the call through, at first she didn't recognize his voice.

"Sheriff's office. How can I help you?"

"Hello, this is Pearl Kelly. I'm the President of the Middle Pass Goat Club and I want to report a theft."

"Hi, Pearl. This is Dan. What happened?"

Pearl had known Sheriff Dan back when she worked at Riverbend Hospital and got reacquainted during his investigation of the murder of her shed boy, Pat. He was also her sole goat milk customer.

"Oh, sorry, I didn't expect you to be working now." Pearl's cheeks burned. "Someone stole a three-month-old goat kid from Lindy Lang's van today during the showmanship competition at the Skunk Cabbage Festival. It was a truck show and her daughter Sierra had left the kid in their van until her turn to show. When she went to get her, the goat was gone."

"Did you notify the festival management?" asked Dan.

"Of course we did!" Pearl's limited patience frayed. "We had their staff check every vehicle leaving the parking lot, as well as staff and others going through the whole park looking for it."

"Sorry, Pearl. I didn't mean to upset you." His words soothed her. "I just wanted the details. I'm sorry the little girl had her goat stolen. The appropriate person to report it, though, is the owner of the goat. I can send paperwork to her or she can call me. Do you have her address?"

Pearl clenched her teeth. *Bureaucracy.* She had little patience for it. "So no one will come out?"

"Pearl, they can fill out the paperwork and we'll keep an eye out for the kid, but there isn't much else we can do at this point. Did anyone see anything?"

"I'm not sure yet, but I have a few suspicions." She planted her free hand on her hip. "I can guarantee I'll find out."

Dan chuckled. "I'm sure you will. For now, the place to start is to get the paperwork filed by Ms. Lang. I apologize but we simply don't have the staff to send someone out right now."

Pearl gulped. She knew Dan wasn't at fault. She felt powerless.

"I'll call Lindy and have her contact you first thing in the morning. Thanks."

"We can talk about this a little more when I come by for milk this week. I'll let you know before I come. And don't go doing anything foolish before we talk, Pearl."

Pearl rolled her eyes. "Well, someone has to do something." She hung up the phone before he could respond.

The gears in Pearl's head were already starting to turn. Something had to be done now if they wanted to find Daisy.

Chapter 7

It had been two days since the goat show and Pearl felt rested and ready to take on the day as soon as she woke. The night before, she had taken a hot lavender bubble bath in the claw foot tub Westin had installed on her back deck the prior fall. That always relaxed her enough to get to sleep: there's nothing as soothing as a hot bath under the stars and giant fir trees. Other than a nightmare that someone dognapped Buckley, she had slept like a log.

She played for a while with Buckley and his newest toy, a large cloth fish with a squeaker. She got tired before he did and got up, ready for chores. At the barn, she counted the goats—something she normally did—but it took on a new urgency now that she knew a goat thief was on the loose. After milking and feeding all the goats, she let the chickens out, and went back inside to eat breakfast and start making phone calls.

After eating she called Lindy Lang, Sierra's mother.

"Do you have news?" said Lindy.

"I wish."

"Did you talk to the Lane County Sheriff's office yet?"

"I called right after I talked to you and they said you had to file the report because the goat belongs to Sierra. He said they can send paperwork or you can go to Springfield and fill it out. If you wait for the paperwork, you're talking about Tuesday or Wednesday till you get it. It's so frustrating that they don't have enough deputies to help us. Anyway, I told him you'd call this morning."

Pearl rocked in her chair. "I have some ideas for finding Daisy and wanted to get together with you and Sarah in the next few days to discuss them. I have faith that we can find her and get her back to Sierra. Can you meet at the Bigfoot Café for lunch on Wednesday? I haven't been there yet. Say 12:30? Or do you think we should talk sometime when Sierra can go? I haven't confirmed anything with Sarah yet."

"I can call her. But let's keep Sierra out of this for now. I don't want to get her hopes up unnecessarily," Lindy said.

"Okay, if that time works for you and you don't hear back from me, consider it cast in concrete. Oh, and if you have a picture of Daisy, bring that, too." Pearl pushed the off button on the phone and plopped on the couch.

Chapter 8

Wednesday morning Pearl pulled into the parking lot of the Bigfoot Café. A neon sign advertising it towered over the business. A metal silhouette of Bigfoot stood next to the side of the building. Pearl shook her head and chuckled to herself, thinking that the new proprietors must be optimistic to have put out the kind of money they must have spent. The parking lot had only a few cars in it.

She opened the screen door and front door and walked into the café. The armadillo motif of the Armadillo Café had been replaced by Bigfoot ornamentation, in every mode of art, as far as the eye could see. Brand new blue coffee mugs with Bigfoot on the side hung from a rack on the wall behind the counter. A metal sign that detailed Bigfoot knowledge hung on the wall next to the door.

Pearl took in the rest of the decorations and went to the dining room section to choose a table for three. Soon Lindy and Sarah came through the door and joined her. A thin man with a limp came out the back door of the kitchen with menus in hand and made his way to the table, smiling.

"Hello," said Pearl. "I'm Pearl, this is Sarah, and this is Lindy. When did you officially open?"

"I'm Sean and my partner, the cook, is Henry. Believe it or not, today is our first day," said Sean. "But we're planning to have a Grand Opening on June 1st. We're going to put an ad in the *Middle Pass Gazette,* so watch for it. We'll have door prizes, Bigfoot merchandise, of course, and free coffee."

"You've done a nice job with this place. That sign outside is amazing! It looks like you spared no expense."

Sean handed them the menus. "This place is our dream. We lived in Elmira for years, but it wasn't until I got the settlement from my car accident that we could even consider buying a small country café. When this one came on the market again, we jumped on it.

"It's nice that we can live in the house in the back and not have to worry about the drive from Elmira. And we're farther into the woods here, so our chance of sighting a Sasquatch is even better than before when we could only look on weekends. I don't know if you were aware of it, but one was seen near Triangle Lake in 1972, and there were two reports in 1981 near Veneta. Of course, with this bad leg I'm a bit limited with hiking, but where there's a will, there's a way." He beamed, standing straighter despite his cane. "Now let me get your water."

"So are you through with kidding yet?" Sarah asked the women.

"We're too new to goats to have bred any this year. If Daisy did well in the show ring, we were planning to breed her in the fall," said Lindy. She lowered her head.

"Don't be discouraged, Lindy. I have a good feeling about finding her," said Pearl. "In terms of breeding, I only bred two this year and my Mini Mancha, Rihanna, is due in a few weeks."

After Sean had delivered their water, they all ordered Bigfoot Greens, a salad mix with avocado, carrot, tomato, almonds, and purple cabbage. Pearl changed the subject to the missing goat.

"I asked you both to come here so we can strategize about finding who took Daisy. I know some people don't think we'll ever find her, but we need to try. And we need to do it right away, because the longer we wait, the less chance we'll succeed." Pearl thought back to the true crime shows she had watched. "I have a few ideas of where to look and figured three heads are better than one.

"First, Westin and I plan to go to the Eugene Livestock Auction this coming Saturday in case someone tries to sell her there. That would be a waste since she has an excellent pedigree; the thief won't get as much money without papers. Anyway, we'll look at all the animals consigned and also let the owners of the auction know the situation so they can keep an eye out for her. Do you have the pictures, Lindy?"

Lindy pulled a large envelope out of her bag and opened it. She took out three different photos, each taken from a different angle. "These are the photos we used for her registration."

Pearl reached for the photos. "If I can borrow those, I'll get some copies made and return them to you. We can leave them with different people, including the auction owners."

"What about using them to make a missing poster and posting that on bulletin boards around town?" Lindy asked. "Sierra and I can do that."

"That's a great idea, Lindy." Pearl's eyes brightened. She handed the photos back to Lindy.

"I spent some time yesterday checking Craigslist in every region of Oregon to see if someone is trying to sell her there. I'm focusing on Eugene, Bend, Corvallis/Albany, and the Coast, although I also checked Portland yesterday. I know there's a chance they could sell her farther away, but I decided to limit it to the closest areas. If either of you want to take on checking in one of those areas, let me know. I don't mind doing it, but it's kind of time-consuming."

"I'll be responsible for Bend and the Coast. I had another idea. What if we call together all the 4-H groups for a meeting where we can show them the pictures and ask them to keep an eye out for us?" Sarah said.

Lindy and Pearl nodded in excitement.

"Your salads, ladies." Sean had wheeled out a cart with their green salads.

Pearl turned to look at him. She had wondered how he would carry them out, with his bad leg. They moved aside so he could put their salads on the table. "Do you need anything else?"

Everyone shook their head no. "Thanks, Sean. These look great," said Pearl. She put her napkin on her lap and poured the container of blue cheese dressing onto her salad.

Lindy put the photos back in the envelope and took a bite of her colorful salad. They ate in silence, other than occasionally praising the food.

Pearl finished her last bite. "Did either of you notice anyone out of place or unusual at the show? I had a weird feeling about a couple of people there." Pearl put her fork on the plate and dabbed at her mouth with her napkin. She took a drink of water before continuing.

"Do either of you know Annie Spink?"

Sarah sighed. "I know who she is but not a lot about her. She's lived in the area for about four years. I did see her right before the show, talking to different people. She spoke to you, didn't she, Pearl?"

"Yes, for a hot minute. She asked some off-putting questions, distracting me when I needed to announce the show. Later, I noticed her walking toward the area where all the cars were parked, but almost immediately put it out of my mind. She left before Sierra discovered Daisy missing. Zora told me she collects animals that other people don't want anymore and she might already have some goats."

"Is there any reason to think she would steal a child's goat, because she appears peculiar?" asked Sarah. "I know she has a farm outside of town and, from what people say, it's a neglected mess. I suspect she doesn't have much money. I can't tell if she's old enough to be getting social security. I don't think she works anywhere around here. Considering the physical condition she's in, if she took Daisy, how would she have gotten out of the festival grounds without someone noticing?"

"I'm suspicious of everyone until I know it couldn't have been them. What do you think about someone paying a visit to her farm, just to make sure?" Pearl looked from Sarah to Lindy. "We could say we needed to ask if she had seen anything out of the ordinary at the show."

"I guess it wouldn't hurt. I can give you directions to her house if you don't mind going," Sarah said.

No danger in going to an eccentric old lady's farm. "Okay. I'll put that on the list," said Pearl.

She finished her salad and pulled out a pad of paper and a pen. "I'm going to start that list of what each of us is responsible for." She wrote as the other two women ate. The only sounds were clattering dishes in the kitchen and the women chewing.

"Other ideas?" asked Pearl.

Lindy raised her hand. "Back to the flyer I'm going to make. What do you think about sending a copy to each of the 4-H families?"

"Great idea!" said Sarah. "That'll save us from trying to coordinate a special meeting."

Pearl dutifully recorded Lindy's suggestion. She laid her pen on the tablet and continued.

"Back to the subject of suspicious people. When I got to the show, Zora and her two sons were there. Zander had a goat to show in the Intermediate class, but Zeus doesn't have goats. He claims not to like them and raises pigs. I saw him and a girl in the parking area looking into car windows before the show. When it ended, Zeus had disappeared. When I asked Zora when he left and where he went, she seemed nervous and tried to avoid the question. She eventually admitted that he had left when the Juniors were showing, but she had no idea where he went. She also told me he came in his own truck. What do you think? Am I being too suspicious? I know she's on the board of the goat club, but what do either of you know about Zeus?"

Sarah and Lindy exchanged looks, and turned to Pearl. "I don't want to say anything negative about any of our 4-H families, but if you have suspicions about him, I think it's worth investigating further," said Sarah. She regarded Lindy with her eyebrows raised. Lindy gave a little nod.

"Do either of you want to volunteer for that?" Pearl chewed on her cheek.

"I barely know her," said Lindy, "so I'm probably not the right person."

"I think you know her as well as I do, Pearl," said Sarah. "And you probably have more time, since I still have a full-time job."

"All right." Pearl shifted in her seat. "I think I'll ask her if I can come over under the pretense of seeing her farm setup. That wouldn't be a total lie." She smoothed her pant legs. Both women nodded.

"Okay, so here's what I have: Lindy is going to make a flyer with the photos and we'll figure out distribution later—except I need some by Saturday for the auction. Sarah will coordinate a mailing to 4-H kids and parents to ask for their help. She'll also keep an eye on Craigslist for Bend and the Coast for any goats for sale that match her description. I'll go to Annie Spink's and Zora's farms, and I'll check Craigslist in Eugene and Albany/Lebanon every day. Westin and I will go to the local auction for the next two weeks, in case the thief tries to sell her. That should do for now. Let's keep in close touch. I think we need to get together for another meeting in a few weeks for an update, if nothing comes out of this. How does that sound?"

Lindy and Sarah said in unison, "Good."

Pearl shoved the notebook and pen back into her purse. Her stomach lurched when she considered going to Zora's farm, but she forced the thought out of her mind as she paid her bill and returned to her car.

Chapter 9

Pearl stared out the window that Saturday morning, marveling at how fast the week had gone. She looked over at Buckley, and back to the front yard where chickens were searching for bugs.

Something caught her eye. On top of the chicken coop sat a gorgeous hawk. She grabbed the binoculars she kept on the end table for bird sightings. She identified a dark cap, reddish orange eyes, small bars on the chest, and larger stripes on the tail before it flew into the air, startled by her movement. She replaced the binoculars and grabbed the bird book, leafing through the section with hawk photos. *A Cooper's hawk.* Her pleasure at observing such a lovely bird evaporated when she thought about her chickens. *Animal thieves everywhere. I'll have to keep an eye on that bird.*

She went to the door, summoning Buckley to come out with her in the hopes that his presence would spook the hawk into staying away from her farm.

With the bird gone, Pearl's mind wandered to the meeting with Lindy and Sarah that week and what she had agreed to accomplish—and had not accomplished so far. She didn't relish the idea of visiting the two farms. The thought of going to Zora's farm caused her heart to start pounding. She didn't trust the woman, and something about her son Zeus unnerved Pearl. She pushed that to the back of her mind and focused on what she would get done. Today they were going to the auction to look for Daisy.

If Westin doesn't show his face soon, I'll have to wake him up.

Lindy had brought her a stack of flyers the day before and she planned to share those with the auction owners. They could go to the auction as late as 11:00, which meant they had less than an hour to get ready.

THEY MANAGED TO GET out the door and leave for the livestock auction by 10:30 am. Westin had answered his door, red-eyed, after Pearl banged on it several times, but he didn't take long to get ready. They both wore their farm clothing and muck boots.

When they arrived at the auction, a few pickup trucks with animals in the back were in line and others were backed up to the weathered wooden corrals behind the building that held a café, an office, and an arena with bleachers. Westin and Pearl went in the front door and stopped to get their bearings. They saw the office behind the door on the left and the café across from it on the right.

"I want to give them these photos and the information on Daisy so they can keep an eye out for her," she said, turning toward the office. Westin followed her.

A red-haired young woman with a western-style plaid shirt and jeans stood behind the counter, which separated the office into two sections.

"How can I help you?" she asked.

Pearl pulled out the flyer with a picture and description of Daisy, and the Langs' name and phone number. "Someone stole this doe kid from the showmanship contest at the Skunk Cabbage Festival last week. We're trying to locate her and figured the thief might bring her here. Would you be so kind as to keep an eye out for her? Maybe keep one of these flyers on the desk so people who come in see it?"

The woman nodded, glancing at the flyer. "I don't always see the animals but I can tape a flyer on the counter here and you can also put some on the bulletin board outside the door. Hopefully someone will come forward with a tip."

"What's even worse is that this goat belonged to a little girl in 4-H. She's devastated. Thanks for your help."

"No problem. Glad to help. Have you thought about trying Craigslist? Lots of people sell goats there. Or on the bulletin boards of the local feed stores?"

"Good ideas," said Pearl. She would have to mention the feed store bulletin boards to Sarah and Lindy. She and Westin turned and walked out the door and into a group of people heading toward the back of the building. Pearl spotted the bulletin board to the left and pinned several flyers onto it. They followed the group, hoping that way would lead them to the arena.

The front seats on the rickety wooden bleachers were set aside for people who would be bidding on the animals. A whiteboard above the area where animals were being brought out and bid on noted that goat sales would start at 1:00. They had arrived too early.

Pearl had another idea. She didn't want to wait around for hours.

"Let's go out and see the animals in the pens in the back. I think we're allowed to do that. They turned and proceeded outside to the back of the building. Following a man and two boys, they let themselves in through a gate and along a winding path of stalls. A cacophony of baas, moos, and maas filled the air and the odor of fresh manure wafted from the pens.

"Since it's past the cutoff time to bring animals in for consignment, we don't even have to watch the auction to find out what goats are here," said Pearl. "Keep your eyes peeled for Nigerian Dwarf goats, particularly a little black and white one."

"Roger," said Westin. He led the way. The goats and sheep were housed in pens before the cattle, so that would make their task easier.

They found four Boer goats in a small pen, agitated and terrified. After that, several pens of skittish, dirty sheep. Two scruffy wether goats with runny eyes stood in the next pen, chewing their cuds.

"There's some Nigerians here," said Westin. He strode toward the pen ahead on the left, with Pearl trailing behind. The back of her throat hurt.

The next three pens were filled with Nigerian Dwarfs, of varying ages. Some were healthy but others sported rough coats and overgrown hooves. Pearl counted 13 of them, but no black-and-white kids. They continued into the dark, dank, and depressing building, with pens alternating sheep and goats, until they got to the pigs.

"I think that's it for the goats." Pearl sighed. "Let's go back."

They turned around, this time with Pearl in the lead. She couldn't get out of there fast enough, but her sadness slowed her pace.

They emerged into the sunlight, squinting as they came out. "Well, that was depressing," said Pearl. She pulled out a tissue and dabbed at her eyes. "Those poor animals."

"Let's go watch some of the auction," said Westin. Seeming unscathed by the dismal tour, he acted like he was on an adventure.

"Okay," said Pearl, "but only for 15 minutes. And I'll have to sit on my hands to keep from trying to rescue one of those pathetic creatures."

They returned to the arena and took seats high in the bleachers. "Be careful you don't get any slivers in your butt," Pearl stage-whispered. "If we sit way up here, we can move our hands without making the auctioneer think we're bidding."

Westin laughed, glad to see that Pearl still had her sense of humor.

They watched the wranglers prod and shove a series of calves into the ring, blocking and hitting them with sticks. Pearl shook her head in disgust. She wouldn't be able to watch this happen to goats. Did they have to be so mean?

During a break in the line of calves being sold someone brought in a cage with a couple of large chickens. *At least the cage will prevent them from being mistreated.*

"I didn't know they auctioned fowl," said Pearl. She fidgeted in her seat, wanting to get out of there before she bought another farm animal. "C'mon, Westin. This is getting too dangerous."

Chapter 10

After a lazy Sunday morning with the *New York Times* and her dog, Pearl decided to visit Jane. She hadn't seen her neighbor for weeks. Pearl wanted to tell her about the goat theft and get her thoughts on how they might find Daisy. Jane's expertise in plants and gardening gave her a different perspective. Pearl hoped she would have some good ideas. She snatched Buckley and walked out the back door, along the path, and over the creek to Jane's house.

Jane knelt on the ground, knees resting on a blue foam knee pad, as she worked in her garden. To her left and right were yellow daffodils, a rainbow of crocuses, and bluebells, among other early bloomers. A bag of fertilizer and a large pile of soil from Lane Forest Products lay on the ground to her side. She watched Pearl approach her.

"Pearl! It's good to see you. I've been so busy, but was going to call if I hadn't heard from you by tomorrow." She stood and gave Pearl an awkward hug, keeping her dirty hands away. "Your visit gives me the perfect opportunity to take a break. I've been out here since after breakfast and my 48-year-old bones starting to feel a little stiff." She laughed. "Come on in for some tea."

Jane led the way up the back steps into her house. Once inside, she removed her green gardening gloves and threw them on top of the washing machine. She continued to the kitchen sink and washed her hands.

Pearl, who knew her way around Jane's house, plopped into a chair at the dining room table and settled Buckley on her lap.

"I need to get your thoughts on a situation that's developed," said Pearl, biting the inside of her cheek.

"Sure. Let me get our tea and get us settled in first. Black tea okay? And would you like a muffin with it?"

"Both sound great to me, Jane." Pearl's eyes lit up at the mention of the muffins. *What a treat.* Jane always seemed to have cake or scones or cookies—a temptation Pearl preferred to avoid.

Jane scurried around the kitchen, boiling water and setting out cups with teabags. She took two raspberry muffins from a recycled bread bag.

Jane brought the tea and muffins to the table on a tray, and sat in the chair across from Pearl's. "Okay. Fill me in. You looked worried."

"Were you aware that someone stole a goat at our showmanship competition during the festival a week ago?"

Jane put a hand on her chest. "No! I guess I haven't seen you in a while. Tell me what happened." She took a small bite of muffin and sat back in her chair.

"It was a truck show, which means that everyone keeps their goats in their truck, van, or crate until it's their turn to show them. A 15-year-old girl named Sierra Lang was supposed to show in the Junior class, but when she went to get her goat out of their truck, it was gone. As you would expect, she didn't take it well. We had to take a break from the show, while everyone spread out and looked for someone with a three-month-old black-and-white Nigerian Dwarf doeling."

"That's terrible. So, the goat wasn't found?" Jane looked concerned.

"No. No luck at all. The show was at the north end of the park, right next to the woods, and the vehicles were all parked there. Lindy Lang, Sierra's mom, had backed the truck in, out of everyone's line of sight, so it's possible that someone took the goat and ran off into the woods with it. Some of the men at the show checked out that area, but it could have been missing for a half hour at that point, so they couldn't find anything other than a few broken branches. I canvassed the whole festival, including the petting zoo—to the best of my ability.

"After I got home, I tried to report it to the sheriff's office, but they told me the owner of the goat had to do it—which wasted valuable time." Pearl scowled and nibbled at her muffin.

"The sheriff's office sent a report form to Lindy to complete. Dan told me that they don't have the staffing to follow through with much of an investigation, though. That was a week ago and since then it's been crickets."

Jane shook her head and tried to suppress a smile. "I think I know where this is headed, Pearl. You want to do the investigation yourself and find the goat."

"Yes," said Pearl, serious. "As a matter of fact, I already met with Sarah, the prior goat club president, and Lindy, to plan strategy. I'm thinking of giving Sierra one of my kids from this year if we can't find Daisy. But I want to at least make an attempt to find her. You were such a help when I was trying to find out what happened to Pat, and I value your opinion, so I wanted to know what you think of our plans or if you have any insight on what kind of person might do this.

"I know you're super busy with your garden at this time of the year and you aren't a goat person, but I want to know if you think I am on the right track."

"What's the plan?" asked Jane.

"We're regularly checking Craigslist and I'm going to a couple of farms. My first thought was to go to the Eugene livestock auction for the next couple of weeks to see if she shows up there. Westin and I went yesterday and had no luck, but we're going back next Saturday. I also left a photocopy of a couple pictures of Daisy with the auction owners and put some flyers on the bulletin board there. The woman running the desk at the auction suggested taking flyers to feed stores. Do you ever go there to get gardening supplies?"

"No, I usually go to garden stores or Fred Meyer for what I need."

"Westin had never been to an auction, so we sat in for about 15 minutes so he could experience it. That was all I could take, though. I felt too sorry for the animals. I don't think the handlers need to be so rough." Pearl picked up the sugar bowl and added a spoon of sugar to her tea, stirring.

"I've never been to an auction, either. No one auctions plants." She guffawed.

Pearl rolled her eyes at the bad joke. "Maybe you should go with me, or Westin, next Saturday. It's something everyone should experience at least once. You just have to wait for the cutoff time on accepting animals, then walk through the stalls looking. It's faster than having to sit through hours of an auction. But if you want to be made uncomfortable, go in and watch the bidding."

"Let me think about it," said Jane. "I'll let you know later this week."

"Okay," said Pearl.

"More tea?"

"Thanks. I'll have another cup. Hey, do you remember Zora Vega, the goat lady I've complained about? Hers is one of the farms I need to check out, but I'm dreading it. The other farm is Annie Spink's. Do you know who she is?"

"I think everyone knows who she is. It's hard to miss her garish clothing and oddness. She's downright weird." Jane grinned and shook her head. "People say her farm is a mess and she has a lot of animals. You'll see what I mean when you go there. I also heard a rumor that she'd been in trouble for animal hoarding somewhere on the coast."

"That's interesting, since people are telling me she collects animals now." Pearl flinched. "I figured a visit wouldn't hurt and would give me a chance to check out her farm. If she has a lot of animals, maybe she thought Daisy would blend in with them."

"That sounds like a realistic possibility. You may be on the right track suspecting her, if the stories about her are true," said Jane. "And besides, it can't hurt to check."

Buckley struggled in Pearl's lap, having reached the end of his tolerance for sitting still.

"Oops, Buckley is telling me it's time to go. Call me later this week to let me know if you decide to go to the auction. I'll keep you informed about what I find at the other farms."

"I'm sorry I can't offer any new ideas for finding the goat, but keep me in the loop. I'm busy with the garden this time of year, but I want to help in any way I can."

Pearl pushed her chair away from the table and stood. "Thanks, Jane. Knowing I have you to rely on is a help." She gave her a hug, with Buckley squished between them.

Chapter 11

More than a week had passed since the goat theft and Pearl was busy with work around the property. She had been avoiding thinking about their plan to find Daisy.

She had trepidation about going to Zora's farm and shuddered when she thought about it. She dreaded being around the woman at all. As the years had gone by, she found her dislike for Zora had increased. Still, she needed to assure herself that the Vegas didn't have Daisy.

Her thoughts turned to Zeus. *Why did he and that girl dress in all black? Why was Zora evasive when she asked where he had gone when he left the show?* Pearl had reason to be suspicious.

She had planned to ask Zora if she could come by to check out her barn setup, but decided instead to drop by unexpectedly. If they had Daisy, they wouldn't have time to hide her if they didn't know she was coming.

The phone rang. It was Jane, asking if she could come over with a bouquet of flowers she had arranged.

"Jane, I'm going to follow one of my hunches about Daisy's thief. I'll be at Zora's farm for about an hour or so. I decided not to give advance notice in case they're hiding her. Is it too late for you to stop by around 8:30? I can even fill you in on how it went." Pearl chewed a cuticle.

"Sure. You know I'm a night owl. Be careful and don't let her get to you."

Pearl laughed. "No worries. I'll call you when I get home."

She took Buckley out for a short walk and afterward got a raw chicken foot out of the freezer to occupy him in her absence.

PEARL PULLED UP TO the Vega residence next to the silver Ford Fusion parked in the driveway. She saw someone peeking out the front curtain. She stepped out of the car and put her hand on her stomach, hoping to quell the nausea. She smoothed her blouse and started for the house. As she climbed the five concrete steps, the heavy wooden door opened and Zora stood there. Pearl couldn't read the expression on her face.

"Pearl, what a nice surprise. What are you doing here?"

Pearl peered over Zora's shoulder into the house, which, as her mother used to say, "looked like a tornado went through it." Magazines, clothing, sports equipment, and junk were piled in various spots. Noticing Zora's eyes narrow jolted her back to her task.

"Um, I was in the area and remembered our talk about seeing each other's barn setups. I hope this is a good time. I've been thinking about building another barn for my bucks, so I'm hoping to get ideas of what other people have done and what tips they have." Pearl chewed her lip for a moment, but stopped herself.

Zora's gaze had softened. "Oh, what a good idea. I should come over to your place sometime to see your barn, too. Let me get my boots on. Go around the house and I'll join you in the back. I'm the only one home today, so it's nice to have the company—especially someone I can talk goats with."

"I was thinking about suggesting a program for the 4-Hers where we could see everyone's setup and offer advice for improvements or share what works and doesn't work. It might even make a good subject for one of our educational meetings," Pearl babbled, catching herself only when Zora closed the door on her.

She turned to the left side of the house where a path led to the back. She walked along the dirt path to the back of the house in time to see Zora coming out the back door with her muck boots on.

I hope she doesn't get suspicious because I didn't wear my muck boots. Pearl rubbed her face and continued on the path.

"I didn't bring my muck boots because I hadn't planned this visit," Pearl lied, "but these sneakers are old, so I don't care about them."

Zora had a blank expression on her face. "Our barn is over here. We have two pastures. Some of the goats are out at the farther pasture browsing for their before-bedtime snack, but I can take you in to see the others." Zora held her head high, smiling, as she led Pearl into the barn.

"This is the main barn. We have it separated with a double row of fencing to keep the bucks from the does, for obvious reasons."

Pearl observed that each side of the barn opened to separate paddocks for bucks and does.

"That's similar to how my barn is set up, too. What do you have for the does and kids?"

"The does get a larger pasture than the bucks, because there are more of them. Also they're milkers, so they get priority." Zora snorted.

Pearl followed her around the barn and into the doe and kid section, which was divided into numerous pens. Pearl had arranged her barn differently because her does lived communally. She got a glimpse of the nearby pasture, which held a few does and older kids. She saw no sign of a black-and-white Nigerian, either inside or out. Two of the larger stalls were full of Nigerian Dwarf kids, but none matched the description of Daisy.

Pearl chewed on her lip. "This is really nice, Zora. Have you sold all your Pygmies?"

"We have a couple of older does in the upper pasture, but I'm phasing them out. I decided I wanted dairy goats, but not full-sized ones. I only kept the old lady Pygmies that I felt obligated to for giving me so many kids."

"Why are all the kids in those two stalls and not with their moms?"

"We pull all the kids at birth so we can milk the moms." Zora crossed her arms over her chest.

Pearl frowned. "I hadn't considered doing it that way. I keep the kids with their dams and start milking after two weeks. Isn't it a hassle, and expensive, to have to bottle feed all those kids?"

"That's the way professional goat dairies do it." Zora stood with her hands on her hips and smirked. "And we have Zanny to do most of the bottle feeding. It's the only way to make them tame, and easier to sell. Some folks wonder why they can't sell their goats, when it's obvious that they're wild from not being handled. We don't drink the goat milk, so we just feed it back to the kids. After the kids are weaned, we use the milk for our feeder calves and the two pigs we raise for ourselves every year."

"Oh, that makes sense," Pearl gave her a weak smile and went still. She could feel her stomach flip-flopping. *Zora's such a know-it-all.* Pearl found bottle-fed kids needy and annoying.

Zora pointed out the open loft above some of the stalls. "Here's where we store our hay."

Pearl nodded. She felt the skin on her lip ripping as she chewed it.

"Want to see our milk room?" asked Zora, oblivious to Pearl's discomfort.

Pearl expected the milk parlor to be a mess like the inside of the Vega house. She was shocked to see an immaculate room. A door kept the goats out and the cement floor had a drain in the middle. A milking machine sat next to the homemade multi-goat milk stand. The far end held a sink and a full-sized refrigerator. Zora opened the refrigerator to show off the milk storage.

Pearl felt a twinge of jealousy. "Zora, this is amazing! Is there anything you can think of that's a downside to your setup?"

"I designed it," Zora said. "And this is the positive part of Zander having OCD—he can't stand a mess. You should see his room." She chuckled. "The only thing I would have done differently would be to make two doors: one for goats coming in and another for those going out, so we wouldn't have to hold back the overeager ones when we let out a doe that's already been milked. That's about it. Do you have any more questions?"

Pearl thought for a minute. "I can't think of any, but I'll call you if I do. Thanks for showing it to me on short notice, Zora. Your farm visit is the trial run for the 4-H program we're thinking about, if we decide to implement it."

Zora brushed at her pant leg. "Someone told me you and Sarah are helping Lindy search for Sierra's goat."

Pearl felt her pulse pounding in her ears and moisture forming in her armpits. *Could Zora know why she came?* "Yes. Why? Do you know anything?"

Zora turned away from her and scratched at peeling paint on the barn. "No. I just wondered."

"I'm going over to Annie Spink's farm this week to check. She acted so strange at the goat show and disappeared around the time Daisy vanished." The words tumbled out of Pearl's mouth before she could stop herself. *What if Zora realized that she was at the Vega farm for the same reason?*

Zora wiped her hands on her pants. "I agree she's an odd one," she said in a monotone voice. "Let's go."

When they stepped outside the gate, Zora pointed out a smaller building with a separate fenced pasture. "That's where Zeus raises his pigs."

Pearl peered over, noticing a few pigs rooting through the destroyed grass. "It's nice you have all these different areas."

Zora led the way back to the house. "Do you want to come in for a cold drink? I just made some lemonade."

Pearl did a double take, surprised at the invitation. "Sure. That sounds nice."

When they got to the front of the house, Zeus was in the yard washing his big black Dodge Ram with a garden hose. Pearl squinted at him, cringing inside. She followed Zora up the steps and into the house. She felt Zeus's eyes on her.

As they made their way through the living room, Zora kicked aside sports gear and clothing to make a path for them, acting as if it was normal. "Have a seat while I get the lemonade."

Pearl sat on the end of the ratty salmon-colored corduroy sofa, pushing aside pillows and a crocheted afghan. Maple end tables and a matching coffee table with a glass top took up the three sides of the couch that weren't against the wall. The tables were a mess of papers, magazines, knickknacks, coasters, remote controls, and used dishes. A pile of bills on the end table, some unopened, beckoned to her. She glanced up to make sure Zora was still in the kitchen and thumbed through them. Chase credit card, electric company, Kohl's, Shell gas, American Express.... Some were second notices. Pearl dropped the mail and put her hands in her lap at the sound of the front door opening.

Zeus shuffled into the house with a grim look on his face as Zora returned from the kitchen carrying two glasses of lemonade and sat next to Pearl. He didn't give either of them a second look as he marched through the living room toward the kitchen.

"Zeus, honey, will you stop for a minute?'

He whirled around, glaring at her. "What's so frickin' important?"

"I wanted you to say hello to Pearl. She stopped by to see the farm setup."

"Hello." He scowled at Pearl and continued to the kitchen.

Zora's neck reddened.

Well, that was rude. And Zora didn't even chide him. What a dysfunctional family.

"Sorry. You know how teenagers are." Zora laughed and elbowed Pearl.

Pearl rubbed her arm. "Other than the goat show, did you see much of the Skunk Cabbage Festival? I had meant to spend some time there afterwards, but I was too upset to do anything but go home."

Pearl shoved aside some magazines and moved a coaster from a pile of junk on the coffee table before setting her glass on it.

"Oh, yeah. Well, we go every year. A lot of it's the same, so it's no big deal to me." Her eyelids fluttered as she spoke.

"I didn't realize Weird Al was playing there the first night or I would have gone. Oh, well, maybe next year," said Pearl.

"We had front row seats. We always go to the concerts they hold. He put on a great show," Zora jutted her chin out, looking smug.

Pearl drank her lemonade, wishing that just once Zora wouldn't have to one-up her. *I have to get out of here.*

"I can't believe what good weather we're having this spring," said Zora.

"Mm hmm." Pearl finished her lemonade and held the glass out. "I have to get going. Do you want me to put this in the kitchen?"

"No, that's fine. I'll take care of it."

Pearl eyed the used glasses, plates, and soda cans on every flat surface in the room. *I'll bet you will.*

"Okay." Pearl stood. "Thanks for the tour and the lemonade."

"Thanks for coming over," said Zora. She stood and reached out, pulling Pearl to her in a bear hug. Pearl tensed and put one arm around Zora self-consciously.

Well, that was awkward. Pearl disengaged herself and exited the house. When she got into her car, she sat for a moment trying to process what had just happened. She finally started the car, backed out the driveway, and returned to the dusty gravel road, disappointed and confused.

Chapter 12

D riving by the side of the Vegas' pasture, Pearl noticed a herd of goats in the distance. Zora had mentioned that not all of her goats were in the barn yet. She peered across the green pasture and saw the herd browsing along the fence line on the far side. Large fir trees shaded the ground between the fence and gravel road. She had an idea. She would drive over to make a final check for Daisy. No one would be the wiser.

She maneuvered along the dusty country road, took a right, and another right when she reached the end of the Vega property. She pulled in under one of the tall firs lining the road and parked. She sat in the car biting her cheek as she surveyed the area. Because of the hill, she couldn't see the Vega house or barn, which meant they couldn't see her, either. The massive acreage across the street from the Vegas' property protected their prying eyes from her, too.

Peering around, Pearl told herself that Tommy and Zander were unlikely to come by her on their way home. She opened the car door, slid out, and walked along the fence line. She could see about 10 Nigerian Dwarf goats—all adults—and a few Pygmies. No kids.

Her mind flashed back to Zeus and the girl skulking around the parking lot. Her stomach fluttered as she conceded to herself that Zeus's creepiness didn't make him a criminal. The disappointment hit her like a sledge hammer. *How could I be so off-base?*

She had to face the fact that everything she had done so far to find Daisy had failed. She had failed. She walked back to the car and reached for the door handle when she heard a noise like a cracking branch. She saw the goats stampeding up the hill toward the barn. *That's odd. What could have scared them?*

Before she could open the door, she saw a flash of black and brown out of the corner of her eye. Clutching the door handle, she turned her head in that direction and saw a German shepherd-like dog lunging at her. Pearl flashed back to what had happened in Ecuador and froze. Everything went black.

Chapter 13

"**P**earl, wake up. Are you okay?" A deep, distant voice seemed to come out of a dream. "Pearl," it said again.

Pearl opened her eyes. Intense blue eyes gazed back at her. It took her a few seconds to realize it was Dan's voice. He knelt beside her with his face close to hers. Her eyes got big and she moved her head back and forth in a panic.

"What time is it? Where am I?" She shuddered as she flashed back to the dog leaping at her. "Is that dog still here?" she asked, looking around in confusion.

"It's a little after 9:00 at night. There's no dog here. How do you feel? Don't sit up too fast." Dan crouched, put his arm around her, and stood, helping her to her feet. "You're next to the far pasture at Zora's. Jane called me and said you'd gone to Zora's but didn't come home and didn't answer your phone when she called. She drove over to your property and talked to Westin, who also had no idea where you were.

"I went to the Vega farm, looking for your car along the way. Zora said you'd left about 8:00. Driving away, I noticed your car over here on the road under the trees. What were you doing here?"

"Let me think. Am I hurt?" She surveyed her body, but saw only dirt and fir needles on her clothing. She didn't feel any pain. Dan still had one arm under her left arm and around her back. She could feel his warmth against her body. Unbidden, her tears fell.

"Oh, honey. It's okay. You seem fine. I think you must have fainted. What's the last thing you remember?"

Honey? Pearl's knees felt weak. Then the dam broke as she tried to hold back sobs. Her thoughts were muddled, and she didn't know why she was crying. As she leaned against Dan, she felt something she hadn't felt in a long time.

"I came over to this pasture to make sure Daisy wasn't in the herd with the goats I noticed over here when I left Zora's. As I reached for the car door the goats started running and I turned around to see a German Shepherd dog about to attack." Pearl felt dizzy as the blood drained from her face.

Dan supported her, then gently let her go but stayed close and watched to make sure she didn't stumble or fall. "We'll sort that out later. For now, you need to get checked out to make sure you don't have a concussion. I want to take you to the emergency room. Let's call Jane and have her bring Westin out here to drive your car home."

Pearl let out a muffled sob. She pulled the driver's side door wider and reached into the car to grab a tissue from the console between the seats. She dabbed at her eyes and steadied herself.

She peeked at Dan, feeling a rush of uncharacteristic shyness. "I feel like such an idiot. I'm fine now, though. I don't need to go to the hospital."

Dan reached out and gave her arm a little squeeze. "You aren't an idiot, Pearl. And you know, as a nurse, that if it was anyone else, you'd insist they get checked out, to be on the safe side."

Pearl brushed at the debris on her clothing. "You're right, Dan," she murmured.

"Is your key still in the ignition?" Dan reached in and got the keys dangling from the ignition and put them under the floor mat. He shut the door and helped her into his patrol car.

He climbed into the driver's seat, pulled out a cell phone, and dialed Jane's number before remembering that the area had no cell phone service. He returned the phone to his pocket and made a U-turn on the road, heading toward town.

They arrived at Riverbend hospital about 35 minutes later. Dan helped Pearl out of the car and they went into the emergency room where Pearl completed the registration process. They sat on yellow faux leather chairs in the lobby to wait until she could be seen by a doctor. Dan pulled out his cell phone and called Jane.

"I found her. She's okay but we're at Riverbend getting her checked out. We left her car on Fisk Road, along the far side of the Vega acreage. Do you know where I'm talking about? Can you take Westin there to get her car, if he's around?"

Pearl sat next to Dan, her mind numb.

"Okay. We'll call when we get home. Thanks so much, Jane."

"Jane's going to pick up Westin and he'll drive your car home."

Chapter 14

They heard Buckley's muffled barking as soon as they pulled in behind her Subaru. They got out of the car and headed for the house. She went inside, reassured Buckley, and turned on the porch light. Buckley had let out a loud yelp and come flying out the door when he saw Dan, mistaking him for a stranger. The hair on his neck stood up and he growled until Dan got closer. Buckley became a different dog, wiggling and jumping on the sheriff's legs.

"I'll bet you're glad to have your mom back." He rumpled the fur on the little dog's neck.

"Did you call Jane to let her know you're okay?" he said to Pearl.

"I'll do it. I'm going to ask her over so I don't have to tell what happened twice. Sit down." She felt better being home.

For the first time she noticed how handsome Dan was. She felt her cheeks redden and went to the kitchen to hide them and fill the kettle for tea. With that done, she went into the living room and called Jane.

"Yes, I'm fine," she said into the phone. "They checked me over and did a CT scan, but found nothing. It was kind of a waste of time."

Dan shook his head and chuckled at Pearl's remark.

"If you can come over now, I'll tell you what happened," she said. "Dan's here and I don't want to have to repeat my story."

She hung up the phone and turned to Dan. "I need to go thank Westin for getting my car. I don't want to share any details with him right now so I'll be back in a second."

"Are you safe to go alone?"

"I'm a little shaky, but I'm sure I can walk that far." Pearl felt her bravado returning.

She went out the front door and came back less than three minutes later. "He's such a great guy," she told Dan. "I rely on him a lot. Not to disparage Pat, but he didn't have all that many skills. Westin can do just about any job around the farm and he also works for Jane on gardening projects."

Dan, with Buckley on his lap, and Pearl sat at the table with their tea. Moments later, Jane knocked and let herself in the door.

"The kettle's on low. I wasn't sure if you wanted anything to drink," said Pearl.

"I'm so glad you're okay," said Jane. "You have no idea how worried I was."

Jane walked to the kitchen, opened the cupboard, and got a peppermint teabag. She put the teabag in the cup Pearl had set out and poured hot water over it, turned off the kettle, and joined them at the table.

"You seem fine, other than the debris on your shirt, Pearl," said Jane. "So what happened?"

Pearl brushed at the fir needles left on her shirt and looked at Dan.

"Dan, I don't think you knew, but one of the people I suspected of stealing Daisy, the goat, was Zora's son, Zeus. There's something sinister about that kid and I'm not talking about the fact that he's left-handed. I saw him and a girl looking in car windows at the beginning of the goat show. They disappeared before it ended. Zora said she didn't know where he went, but she acted evasive. So I wanted to make a surprise visit to their farm to see if I could find Daisy there." She shook her head, remembering back.

"Needless to say, the visit was a failure. No Daisy. Still, on the positive side, I got to see how Zora's barn was set up and learn more about her goat management. It's very different from mine. Anyway, when I turned on her road to come home, I remembered that she said she had let another part of her herd into the farthest pasture. I decided to drive around and see if Daisy might be with them.

"I parked by the fence under some trees along the far road, where I knew Zora wouldn't be able to see me. I got out to get a better view of the goats in that pasture and as I started to open my car door, something startled them and they ran back to the barn. I glanced to the side and saw a large German Shepherd lunging at me. That's all I remember until Dan came along and found me."

Jane put her hand over her mouth. "Thank goodness you weren't hurt! But how? If the dog didn't attack, what happened to you?"

"That's the thing. As the dog came at me, I had a flashback to an incident that had happened to me in the Peace Corps in Ecuador." Pearl's hands shook. She clutched them in her lap.

"When I got there," said Dan, "there was no sign of a dog."

"Now I'm not even sure if there *was* a dog tonight. Could I have hallucinated it? It seems so surreal now when I talk about it." Her voice trailed off.

"Dan, would you mind if I held Buckley?" she said.

"Not at all." He passed the little dog to Pearl.

Chapter 15

Pearl spoke slowly as she stroked her pup. "In 1986, Christopher Rhodes and I met as volunteers in the Peace Corps, assigned to a small village in Ecuador. In a short time we were crazy in love with each other."

Pearl's gaze shifted up as she replayed the memory in her mind. She shook her head to bring herself back to reality, and returned to her story. "Anyway, we had gotten engaged a few days earlier. Christopher and I were riding a motorbike to the Rio Pita waterfalls, when out of nowhere came a German Shepherd-like dog. It rushed at us, snapping. I was on the back of the bike and closest to it but lifted my legs so it couldn't reach me. At the same time, Christopher tried to kick it away. He connected with the dog's head on the second try. The vicious thing fell, stunned, and we raced away. Chris didn't realize he'd been injured, but when we got to the waterfall and took off our shoes and socks to wade in the water, he noticed a wound on his ankle. It was so small that it didn't even need a bandage. Physically, he seemed fine, and we forgot it even happened."

Pearl had a haunted look in her eyes. "*He* felt fine, but I began to wake up screaming from nightmares about the dog attacking me. I think it was an omen."

Pearl clutched Buckley tighter. She closed her eyes and shook her head, trying not to react to the memories.

She swallowed hard. "Two weeks later, Christopher was sick, with a fever, headache, and stomach problems. We thought he had gotten food poisoning from eating at a street cart, something that had happened to both of us before. He stayed in bed for several days, but the sickness didn't go away like it usually does with food poisoning." Her voice trailed off as she remembered.

She stared at her hands. "He got worse. We went to the local health clinic, where he had a seizure, and they had him transported to the hospital. I never saw him again. He died two days later."

Pearl's eyes filled with tears. She handed Buckley back to Dan and jumped up to busy herself in the kitchen.

Dan and Jane exchanged glances. "Do you want any help?" said Jane.

"No, I have everything under control. Do either of you want to try the goat cheese I made? I have some rice crackers to go with it." Without waiting for an answer, she went to the refrigerator and pulled out the cheese. She got a few butter knives from the drawer and filled a small plate with crackers. She took everything to the table, holding her tears at bay. She continued to pace in the kitchen.

Her friends exchanged concerned looks. They each took a knife and tried the cheese, to give her some emotional space.

"This is delicious, Pearl," said Dan. "Hopefully you'll start selling it along with the milk. I would certainly be a customer."

"Amazing," said Jane. "I love it."

Pearl hugged herself and sat at the table to eat some cheese and crackers. Dan scrutinized her face as she chewed on her cheese and cracker. He didn't want to push her too far but still had questions.

"How did they figure out that rabies killed Christoper?" he asked.

Pearl held onto the table in front of her. "After he died, the doctors called to tell me that one of the tests they did came back positive for rabies virus. They'd been seeing a lot of it there. They asked about exposure to a bat or a vicious dog. Then I remembered the dog attack. I felt guilty because I'd been having nightmares and should have figured out that they were some kind of unconscious signal that he had rabies."

Pearl looked at the ceiling as though remembering. She lost her composure again and sobbed.

Dan handed her a clean cotton handkerchief from his pocket and rubbed her back until her tears subsided. She wiped her eyes and took a deep breath.

"We had a ceremony at the village where we were staying. His parents had his body shipped home for burial. I spent the next few weeks overwhelmed with grief and blamed myself. If only we had reported the bite right away. If only he hadn't kicked at the dog. If only I would have realized that the dog might have rabies...." Her voice trailed off.

Pearl sat at the table, pensive. Jane had tears in her eyes. Dan put his hand on Pearl's arm. "I'm so sorry you had to go through that," he said. She could feel his warm hand on her arm, as though he was absorbing some of her pain.

Pearl felt dazed. "The if-onlies can drive a person crazy. I left my assignment in Ecuador before it officially ended. I couldn't think and was of no help to anyone in the village. I went home for a short while, but spent the next five years traveling. Now I believe I was running from my feelings."

She paused. "So that's my story. I'm sorry to be such a downer. I haven't talked about it in almost 40 years. It's weird how that German Shepherd at Zora's, if it even existed, took me right back there."

"You aren't a downer, Pearl," said Jane. "And I think the dog *was* there. I'm glad you felt safe to share your story with us."

They sat without speaking for a few minutes, crunching as they ate their crackers and cheese. Jane checked her watch.

"I need to get going. It's past your bedtime, Pearl." She stood and Pearl followed suit. Jane put her arms around Pearl in a long embrace. "I'll talk to you tomorrow. And call me anytime."

Jane retrieved the cheese plates, the knife, and the tea cups and carried them to the sink. She walked to the front door to leave.

Dan stood as Jane opened the door. "Goodnight, Jane," he said. "And thanks again for calling me tonight."

He put Buckley on the floor and turned his attention to Pearl. "I'd better get going, too. I have to work early tomorrow. Will you be okay?"

Pearl nodded. He gave her arm another squeeze and turned to leave. Pearl felt emotionless and dead on her feet.

"Oh, I almost forgot. I have a clean jar in the car and $7.50 in my pocket. Do you have any milk for sale?"

Pearl nodded. Her eyes were puffy and her brain felt fuzzy.

"Be right back," he said. He went out the front door.

A moment later he came in with an empty half-gallon jar and put that and $7.50 on the table. "Thanks! Best goat milk in Oregon."

That elicited a weak smile from Pearl.

"Good night, Dan," she said, as she finished clearing the table. She held out the jar of milk.

He came over and gave her a hug before he took the jar and walked out the door. "Take it easy for a few days and don't try to save the world." He winked at her and walked out to his car, clutching the jar of milk.

Chapter 16

Pearl had taken Dan's advice and spent the next two days relaxing, taking hot baths, and reading—besides doing daily chores. Spring, her favorite season, was in full bloom, or at least well on its way. The purple lilac bush Westin had planted next to the house had budded and she could already smell its heavenly fragrance.

She worked hard not to beat herself up over Daisy getting stolen. Every time she had negative thoughts about it, she focused on her goats, which made her happy. She also got a warm feeling when she thought about Dan and the possibility that their friendship could be more. She had even treated herself a pint of coffee ice cream before bed the night before, calorie counting be damned.

Today she felt ready to get going again. Pearl lugged the day's milk to the house when she met Westin, humming "I Lost on Jeopardy."

She set the milk container on the ground. "Weird Al, right? He was at the Skunk Cabbage Festival and no one told me!"

"Yeah, I went. He puts on a great show," said Westin. "I wish I had gotten there earlier so I could get a better seat. I mean, *a* seat. I had to stand in the back."

"You were there?" She thought for a minute. "Why didn't you tell me?"

Westin shrugged. "I don't know. I guess it didn't occur to me that you might be a fan."

"Did you see anyone you knew there?"

Westin nodded. "Dave, from the Pub, and Zora and Tommy Vega. There was a huge crowd."

"Zora told me they were in the expensive seats."

Westin guffawed. "No. They were behind the roped off area, just like me."

"I don't know why she has to lie about everything." Pearl put a finger in the air. "Oh, yeah. Just so you know, I'm visiting Annie Spink's farm in a few hours. I want to get back to putting my energy into finding Daisy."

Westin tilted his head, frowning. "Who's Annie Spink?"

"A weird woman I met at the goat show. She'd vanished by the time we knew Daisy had been taken. Zora told me she collects misfit farm animals and Jane told me she'd been in trouble for animal hoarding in the past."

Westin leaned toward her, grasped her arms, and stared into her tired blue eyes. "Don't push yourself. And make sure to be careful, and *don't* make any bad decisions. I'll check on Buckley in a few hours and let the chickens out at noon, like usual. Come and get me when you get back, in case I'm inside or out in the field. I don't want anything else going wrong."

Pearl relaxed a little. She scoffed, "I don't think there's anything to be careful about. She's just an eccentric old lady."

Westin shrugged and put his hands in his pockets. "Okay, Wonder Woman."

Pearl picked up the stainless-steel milk transfer can. "I shouldn't be gone long. I figure if I don't give her warning before I go, she won't be able to hide the goat if she has it."

Westin stroked his chin and grimaced. "I'm getting déjà vu. As I recall, that was your plan when you went to Zora's, and look how that turned out."

She sighed. *Will I ever live down "the accident" at Zora's?*

"Like I said, Annie's just an eccentric old lady."

Westin walked away, shaking his head.

It wasn't Pearl's fault that someone stole Daisy. Part of her didn't want to deal with anyone, but she had made a commitment, which included investigating Annie. Besides, she told herself, who better to do it than a nurse. She had taken care of lots of people with mental health issues.

Pearl carried the milk to the house, slipped off her muck boots on the front porch, and entered the front door, being careful not to trip over the waggling dog that greeted her. She put the milk on ice to chill it quickly. She went back to the mud room and removed her coveralls.

She had no appetite but needed to feed Buckley, at least. She poured some kibble into his bowl and gave him fresh water. She settled on the couch with her second cup of coffee and a piece of buttered, sprouted-wheat toast while Buckley crunched on his kibble, one piece at a time.

Pearl puzzled over what to expect from the peculiar woman. She picked a piece of loose hay from one of her socks and put it in a bowl on the coffee table. After learning that Annie might be an animal hoarder, Pearl's curiosity had been piqued—not only regarding the theft but the woman herself. Because of her interest in people she had once heard someone refer to as "social weeds," she had originally planned to specialize in psychiatric nursing. That plan was waylaid when she found that emergency medicine provided the variety she needed in her work; but she hadn't lost her fascination with underdogs.

Buckley finished his food and jumped up beside her. He nuzzled the hand holding her coffee cup, causing coffee to slosh out the side onto the floor. She put the cup on a coaster and sopped the coffee up with a napkin.

Buckley pressed into her side and she caressed his soft fur. Despite being a pain in the neck, the little guy always had a way of making her feel good.

An hour later Pearl was in her car heading for the Spink farm.

Chapter 17

Pearl pulled in the driveway at Annie's farm. She gaped in disgust as she took in the surroundings. Years of neglect had left the grass in the front yard overgrown. It didn't appear to have ever been weeded. Himalayan blackberry closed in on all sides. Herb Robert, an invasive plant often called "stinking Robert" due to its offensive odor, snaked over an abandoned front lawn, and a variety of thistles reared their stickery but beautiful purple heads.

The condition of the old farmhouse made it look uninhabitable. The glass in a front window had been replaced by cardboard. The house listed to one side and sage green paint had peeled away, exposing bare wood. Pearl hoped Annie's menagerie got better care than the house.

She got out of the car and walked toward the crumbling dwelling, tottering along the broken sidewalk that led to the porch. She crept up the stairs, clutching the rotting handrail, cautious of where she stepped for fear one of the steps might collapse.

She reached the top of the porch, steeled herself, and knocked on the door. Dogs barked inside but no one answered. She knocked again, this time harder. The barking grew louder, but still no answer. Pearl found the doorbell and pushed on it several times. She couldn't hear it ring through the door, but gradually the barking stopped. *What should I do now?*

She descended the front steps and stood surveying the yard. A rusted red pickup truck overtaken by blackberry bushes sat on what must have once been a driveway alongside the steps. *Annie could use some of those goats out here.*

She saw a path on the right side of the house. *Maybe Annie's out back with her animals.* Pearl walked along the path toward the back yard calling out, "Annie. Are you out there?"

Still no response. She stopped at the gate that separated the side from the back yard.

"Annie!" she yelled over the gate. Silence.

Pearl unlatched the gate and let herself into the back yard. She studied the area. The two-acre pasture in front of her hadn't been mowed, but the animals had managed to overgraze it in a few areas. About 20 feet from the house to her right sat a half-century old, rickety wooden barn. In front of it, a small flock of chickens—mostly roosters—were scratching at the ground. *Zora was right about her taking reject animals.*

Pearl walked toward the barn, calling out Annie's name as she proceeded. She watched a few fat gray rats scurry under the side of the building as she approached. She got to the wide, open barn door and peeked inside. It was dark as a coal mine, but as she moved inside her eyes adjusted. The smells of hay and manure became stronger the farther in she walked. In the corners were cobwebs covered with dust. She could see a handful of water buckets hanging from bucket hooks, several feeders half full of hay, and a shovel and a pitchfork suspended from the wall. Stacked along another wall were at least a dozen grimy cages. Pearl looked closer and saw that they were full of rabbits. She stumbled back, feeling unable to breathe.

"Oh, poor bunnies!" She felt an urge to open the cages and let them out. She'd have to quiz Annie on how she cared for them. She could use a good book on raising rabbits, or a report to animal control.

"Annie?" Pearl yelled into the recesses of the barn.

Not even the rabbits broke the silence.

Pearl walked back out into the sunlight and saw a herd of animals headed her way. She saw that there were seven goats, at least ten sheep, two pot-bellied pigs, a horse, a donkey, and a llama. Pearl had come prepared. She had worn her farm clothes, and reached into her pocket to get some of the peanuts she regularly carried. She continued toward the mixed herd, hoping to lure them to her. Some of the animals turned and ran away as she approached, but the donkey and all but two of the goats came her direction.

"I have peanuts, you guys," she said, holding one between her thumb and index finger.

The furry gray donkey came forward and took the peanut with his lips. The poor creature had some kind of mange on its side and back, with patches of fur missing and a section of dark mane missing. Pearl reached out to pat him on the back of his neck and he jerked away.

The other animals that had stuck around pushed closer. Pearl took out the rest of the peanuts and tried to give each animal one, as she attempted to move past them into the pasture.

"Annie! Are you out here?" she yelled. No answer.

What appeared to be a pile of bright-colored clothing a few feet from the back fence caught her eye.

Chapter 18

She strode toward the clothing, the donkey trotting behind her. As she neared the bundle, she gasped in surprise and her hand flew to her mouth. Annie lay face up in the pasture. Pearl's heartbeat quickened and she raced to Annie's side.

"Annie!" she called as she neared her. No answer.

She crouched next to Annie and shook her arm. It was stiff and as cold as a rock. Both her fists were clenched and one held a clump of dark brown hair.

"Annie, can you hear me?" she said, a futile gesture.

She reached for Annie's wrist and felt for a pulse. Nothing.

Pearl saw drying blood in the top of Annie's tousled hair and a pool on the ground under her head. Her head had a slight indentation where she may have been struck with something.

She pulled out her cell phone, put it on speaker, and punched in 9-1-1. She listened for ringing, but heard only silence. She pushed the button to end the call and checked the phone. No bars. She realized that Annie lived too far out for a cell phone to connect to a tower.

Pearl turned and sprinted toward the house to find a landline phone. She tried the back door and was relieved when it opened. Two barking dogs—a chihuahua and a terrier mix—greeted her. The chihuahua continued to yap at a distance, but the terrier jumped on her legs, tail wagging.

"Down!" she said. She reached out and gave the terrier a quick pat on the head, then focused on the task at hand. She rushed through the kitchen searching for a phone. Nothing. The next most logical place was the living room. She raced in there, followed by the two curious dogs, and spied the phone on the table next to the sofa, which had two cats sitting on its back. She rushed over, grabbed the phone, and dialed 9-1-1.

The operator answered immediately. "Lane County 9-1-1. What is your emergency?"

"I need to report a death at the Spink Farm. The body's in the back pasture at the end of Amy Road. I'm not sure of the exact address. The EMTs will have to come in the gate on the right side of the house," said Pearl.

"What's your name?"

"Pearl Kelly."

"What number are you calling from?"

"I don't know. It's a landline that belongs to the victim. There's no cell service here."

"Do you know the victim?"

"Her name is Annie Spink."

"Do you have any idea what happened?"

"She appears to have a head injury. That's all I know."

"Are you able to do CPR? Would you be willing to try that?"

"No. There's no need for CPR. She's dead."

"Is she still breathing?"

"No! I already checked and she isn't breathing, she has no pulse, and is cold and stiff," said Pearl, exasperated.

"I can walk you through CPR if you'd like to try."

"I'm a nurse. I used to teach CPR, so believe me when I tell you it's too late in this case."

"Okay, ma'am. I have officers and an ambulance on the way. Do you have a cell phone number in case I need to call you back?"

"Like I said before, I'm calling on a landline because there's no cell service here. Now I'm going back to the body." Her lips were pressed into a tight line as she ended the call.

"Don't worry, guys," she said to the dogs and cats. "Something happened to your mom and I'm going to go back out with her."

She hurried out the door to Annie and waited for the ambulance.

Time slowed to a snail's pace. Pearl sat next to Annie and some of the animals settled in beside them—except the pigs, who rooted around near the fence. Two chickens walked behind them, scratching and pecking the uprooted areas for worms and bugs.

Pearl spied a plastic-handled hammer with what appeared to be blood drying on its steel face. Pearl surmised that someone had hit Annie over the head and thrown it to the side before leaving. *Who could be so vicious?*

She stood and pulled out her cell phone, glad it had some utility. She walked closer to the hammer and took several pictures, intending to make sure that the sheriff had some evidence of what had occurred. She turned and took a photo of Annie's body.

She parked herself near the body and waited for the paramedics and sheriff.

Chapter 19

Ten minutes later, the distant wail of a siren grew louder and then stopped. Muffled conversation came from the front of the house. The gate latch clicked and two male paramedics walked toward Pearl carrying a stretcher and their trauma kit. She waved them over to where Annie's body lay. It didn't take them long to come to the same conclusion as Pearl had—Annie was indeed dead.

Pearl went to wait by the gate while the paramedics stayed with the body until the sheriff's deputies arrived. She led the deputies out back to the pasture area where Annie's body lay. Annie's barnyard pets had left the area, wandering off in different directions.

After a brief discussion with the deputies, the paramedics went out front to wait for the medical examiner and transport the body after law enforcement had completed the investigation.

The male deputy went back out the gate. The female deputy pulled out a notepad and pen and turned to Pearl.

"Hi, Pearl. I'm Deputy Deatherage, in case you don't remember me. The other officer is Deputy Colton. The paramedics said you found her?" she said. "I'd like to get some information on the victim. What is her name and age?"

"Her name is Annie Spink. I have no idea of her age."

"Is she a friend of yours?"

"She was more an acquaintance than a friend. I'd only met her once before. When I knocked on the front door and she didn't answer, I came out back to look for her and found her body."

"Why were you here, if you weren't friends?"

"I wanted to talk to her. We had a baby goat go missing at the 4-H showmanship competition during the Skunk Cabbage Festival and she was in the vicinity at the time."

"Oh, yeah. I heard about that. Was it your goat?"

"No, but I'm the president of the Middle Pass Goat Club. Some of us are trying to get the little girl's goat back to her. The mother already filed a report with the Sheriff's office. Anyway, I came over to find out if she saw anything. Or if the goat was here."

"Why did you think the goat might be here?"

"Just a hunch. I'd seen her out by the trucks a little while before we found out Daisy was gone. *And* she was asking strange questions."

Deputy Deatherage pursed her lips and continued writing. "Did you see anyone else here when you arrived?"

"I didn't see anyone. I did go in the house to make the 9-1-1 call because there's no cell service here, but didn't see or hear anyone there either, other than the dogs and cats."

Deputy Colton returned with yellow crime scene tape to secure the scene. Pearl and Deputy Deatherage glanced at him as he walked by but said nothing.

"I found her lying right there, just like she is," said Pearl, pointing at the area where the body lay. "I checked for respirations and a pulse, then called 9-1-1. It's obvious she'd been dead for a while. She has a wound on the top of her head and I noticed that hammer over to the right of the body. If you inspect it, you'll see there is what appears to be blood on one end. Don't worry, though. I didn't touch anything and I also took some pictures to help preserve the scene for you. I was afraid the paramedics might do something that would disturb things." Pearl bit the inside of her cheek.

"Do you have any idea of who might have done this?"

"Like I said, I barely knew her."

Deputy Colton finished wrapping the crime scene tape in an area from the trees to the fence and joined them. Deputy Deatherage furrowed her brow and continued writing on the notepad.

She glanced at Pearl. "Is there anything else you want to tell me?"

"No," said Pearl.

"Okay, Ms. Kelly. We're going to have to detain you for now. Please turn around and put your hands behind your back," said the male deputy.

"What the...? Can you at least put the cuffs on in front? I'm old and don't need this. I'm not going anywhere." Pearl stammered.

He glanced at the female deputy who nodded her head. "Okay."

Pearl shook her head in disgust. She held out her wrists and Deputy Colton snapped handcuffs on them.

Deputy Deatherage took her by the arm and escorted her to the back porch. "You can sit here for now. Someone will come and talk to you after we're done."

Pearl took a seat on the porch steps. She eyed her wrists in disbelief. *No good deed goes unpunished.*

Deputy Deatherage turned and walked back to the crime scene. Pearl watched her trying to keep the animals at bay after the donkey attempted to get too close. She shooed him away. She continued to run interference with various goats and the donkey.

Over the next half hour the Sheriff, the medical examiner, and two investigators arrived and joined the officers by Annie's body. The sheriff looked at her handcuffed wrists and shook his head in exasperation when he passed by.

A few minutes later the deputies approached Pearl.

"Sheriff says you can go home now," said Deputy Colton. "They'll want to interview you later at the office."

Deputy Colton removed the handcuffs. Pearl rubbed her wrists and looked at him with narrowed eyes. *Nothing like overkill.*

"If you can think of anything that may be helpful, don't hesitate to call me or one of the detectives. Here's my card."

Pearl went out the gate and to her car. She pulled out her keys when a deep voice called out, "Excuse me, ma'am." She squinted into the sun and held up her hand to block it as she turned. To her right stood an old man with a scruffy beard wearing tattered denim overalls.

Chapter 20

Pearl dropped her hand and raised her eyebrows. "Do I know you?" she asked.

He walked toward her. "No. Can you tell me what's going on over here? I saw all the police cars and ambulance. Did something happen to Annie?"

"Are you a friend of hers?" Pearl wanted to find out how well he knew her before shocking him with the news that she had found Annie's body.

"Neighbor," he said.

"Oh. Well, I found her body out in the pasture."

"Oh, my goodness. She was fine yesterday, showing me the new goat kid she'd got."

"Did she tell you what kind it was?"

"I think it was a dwarf pygmy. It was black and white. She said I could bring my granddaughter over to see it sometime. The granddaughter still talks about when Rooty was a piglet." He chuckled.

Pearl scanned the area and lowered her voice. She knew Dan wouldn't be happy with her interviewing a witness before he did. "Did you see or hear anything unusual around that time?"

"No, I don't think so." He paused a minute. "I take that back. I heard some arguing."

"Did you recognize Annie's voice? What were they saying?" she asked.

"I couldn't tell you if it was a man and a woman or two women. And I certainly couldn't understand anything they were saying. They sounded angry, ya know what I mean?"

"Okay," said Pearl. "Anything else?"

He rubbed his beard. "I heard a car leaving after the argument. I'd gone back in the house and by the time I got outside all I could see was the rear of a gray car driving away."

"Make sure to tell the sheriff what you told me. He and the detectives are out in the pasture right now. But they don't want anyone back there while they're doing the investigation. I imagine they'll want to talk to you and other neighbors. If you want to wait around, you can make sure to tell them what you saw."

He pulled a cigarette pack and lighter out of his pocket. "Do you know what'll happen to her animals? She has a lot of 'em." He extracted a cigarette and lit it.

"I guess they'll call Animal Control and have them deal with it," said Pearl. "You could ask the sheriff. They'll also have to find out if she has any family who could take them. It's the rabbits I'm worried about. It's inhumane to keep them in those small cages." Pearl grimaced and shook her head.

"Rabbits?" He took a deep drag off his cigarette.

"Yeah. She has a bunch of rabbits in cages in the barn." Pearl waved away the cloud of smoke that came out of his mouth.

The farmer scratched his balding head with his empty hand. "That's the first I've heard of it."

"Well, when you talk to law enforcement, tell them about it and I will, too. I've got to get going now." She turned back to her car and got in.

Still distracted by the thought of those poor rabbits, she had to swerve to avoid hitting a possum when she turned onto the highway.

"Focus," she said to herself.

She pulled into her driveway, feeling relieved. She still had half a day to go and already felt overwhelmed.

Chapter 21

Pearl had expected a call from the Sheriff's office the next day, but they didn't call until Thursday. That gave her a day to recover, as well as figure out her next steps.

After a morning phone call from a detective and a light lunch, Pearl attempted to look more presentable, changing into a clean, unstained T-shirt and even putting on a bra before leaving for the Sheriff's Department in Springfield.

When she arrived, the receptionist escorted Pearl to a small room with a table and four cheap metal-and-plastic chairs. Four plastic bottles of water sat on the formica-topped metal table and a mirror covered one wall. The air in the room felt stale, with a slight odor of cigarette smoke.

Pearl twirled a strand of her freshly-washed dark curly hair and eyed the mirror, trying to determine whether it was one- or two-way. After a few minutes the Sheriff and a detective entered the room and joined her at the table.

"Good afternoon, officers," she said. "Are you taking the goat theft seriously now?"

Dan smiled. "Maybe. A murder investigation takes priority over goat thefts, though. This is Detective Corman. He's the lead on this case, so he'll be interviewing you. I came to observe and assist, because of the possible link to the other theft—which was my case."

Corman leaned back in his chair. "I'm not convinced the two thefts—if there were actually two—are related. We have no evidence that the person who killed Annie also took a goat."

Pearl glared at him. "Someone took one of her goats. What do *you* think the motive for the murder was?"

He shrugged. "We don't know. But I'm not sure that stealing a goat kid is motive enough for murder. Why do you think someone stole one of Annie's goats?"

"The neighbor said she'd gotten a new black-and-white kid. For all I know it was Daisy!" Pearl declared. "And there's no goat matching that description on the property now. All the goats there are adults, and the neighbor said she had eight, but I only counted seven. I think there's a connection."

Dan cut in, "We'll investigate that. We need to consider all the circumstances and evidence. We have what we believe is the weapon but still have to wait for DNA results. As you are aware, these things take time. The detectives still have a lot of work to do."

Pearl felt her blood pressure rising. Dan reached over and touched her arm. "We're not on opposite sides."

She swallowed, feeling heat rising on her neck. "You know how focused I get...."

Dan's chuckled and his eyes softened. "Yes, I do."

He moved his hand to his lap and turned to Detective Corman, "Detective, the interview is all yours now." His expression became serious and he pulled a notepad and pencil from his pocket.

"Tell me about that day. When and why were you at Annie Spink's place?"

Pearl relaxed and leaned back. "I was following up on the theft of Sierra's goat at the Skunk Cabbage Festival. Dan can fill you in on that, if he hasn't already."

The detective nodded and scanned the paperwork.

Pearl ran her left hand through her hair. "Right before the goat showmanship competition, I saw Annie going from person to person asking questions. She eventually got to me and asked a bunch of inappropriate questions about goats and the show. She claimed to have raised prize-winning goats, but if that was true, she should have known the answers. I found her to be a nuisance. And then she was nowhere to be found when the goat went missing.

"After I had time to think about it, I remembered what I'd observed at the goat show and considered her a person of interest. I'm an excellent judge of character." Pearl sat straight and stared at the detective.

Detective Corman stopped writing. He raised his eyebrows and returned her stare, then turned to Dan, who shrugged.

Pearl ignored him and continued, "When I asked my neighbor Jane what she knew about the woman, she said she'd heard that Annie had been in trouble in the past for hoarding rabbits somewhere on the coast. And another 4-H mom, Zora Vega, told me that she collects misfit animals. Those two facts only added to my suspicions, so I decided to make an unannounced visit to her farm to see if she had Daisy."

"That reminds me." Pearl's lips curled in disgust. "When I looked for Annie in the barn, I found cages stuffed full of rabbits. Did anyone get them out of there?"

"Yes," said Dan. "Animal Control got a volunteer crew together to take all the animals until any next of kin could be located."

"When did you get to Annie's?" said the detective, not missing a beat.

"Around 11:00 in the morning. It took me 10 or 15 minutes to find her body and call 9-1-1."

"Did you see anyone else there or in the area?"

Pearl shook her head. "No. I assume you talked to the neighbors?"

"We're canvassing the area and plan to interview them."

"The farmer next door told me he heard arguing earlier," said Pearl. "Make sure you talk to him."

Detective Corman scoffed.

Pearl leaned toward him and blinked. "Is the story about rabbit hoarding true?"

Detective Corman looked to the Sheriff.

"I can answer that." Dan cleared his throat. "She was convicted for first- and second-degree neglect of numerous animals, mostly rabbits, in Newport. And it wasn't the first time she'd been cited. One condition of her probation was that she not own any animals for seven years. She seems to have gotten around that by moving to Lane County, buying a farm, and starting to do the same thing."

Pearl took one of the water bottles, unscrewed the cap and took a gulp to relieve the lump in her throat. "Poor animals."

She felt a wave of sadness and closed her eyes, quiet.

The detective glanced up from his notebook. "Did you go in the house?"

"Yes. I needed to find the phone and call 9-1-1."

"So that's the only place we'll find your fingerprints?"

Pearl felt a flash of fear. *What did I touch?*

She thought for a minute, retracing her steps. "The doorknob and the phone. I didn't touch anything else."

"Can you think of anyone else we should talk to?"

Pearl bit her lip. "Other than the neighbors, I also have suspicions about Zora Vega's older son, Zeus, and his girlfriend."

"Why's that?" said the detective, smirking.

Pearl recoiled. "Something about him gives me the creeps. They were dressed in all black and casing vehicles in the parking lot during the showmanship competition at the Skunk Cabbage Festival before Sierra's goat went missing. They mysteriously disappeared before the end of the show, too."

The detective chuckled. "Okay. What's the girlfriend's name?"

"I have no idea."

"I'll add Zeus to the list of people to interview and track down the girlfriend. But lots of kids dress in black."

Pearl glared at him. "I know that. But you asked who else you should talk to."

Detective Corman put his pen on top of the notebook and sat back in his seat, staring at Pearl.

Dan massaged the back of his neck. "Is there anything else you can think of that might be helpful?"

Pearl frowned and rubbed her chin. "No. I was concerned about Annie's animals, and whether she had relatives who could take them—but I take it you aren't aware of any."

Dan shook his head. He closed his notebook and put it and his pencil in his pocket.

Chapter 22

Pearl sat upright, with a jolt, from her resting place on the couch, startling Buckley, who stared at the door, growling and barking.

"Chill out, Buckley! There's no one here."

His barking slowed, then stopped, and he hopped back on the couch next to Pearl.

That Friday evening she had remembered, with dread, that she had agreed to go to the auction with Westin the next day. She hoped Jane wouldn't mind going instead.

She thought the trip would be futile, but didn't want to mention it to anyone. *Why had she even believed someone would be dumb enough to take a stolen goat to a local auction? If they wanted to make money, they'd do better taking it to California, where auction prices are higher.* She would keep her mouth shut because she had made a commitment to Lindy and Sarah and wanted to uphold it.

Besides, since Jane had never been to an auction, it would be an opportunity for her to have a novel experience—like Westin had done the week before. *I'm not shirking my duty. I'm delegating so I can handle more important matters.* Pearl dialed Jane's number.

"Hey, Jane. I'm calling to confirm that you're planning to go to the auction with Westin tomorrow. I just remembered and realized we hadn't reconnected since we talked about it. I'm too busy to go, so I'd hoped you could go with him."

"I haven't talked to Westin either, but I do want to go. It'll be a nice change of pace," said Jane. "Will you verify it with him since he doesn't have a phone?"

"Sure." Pearl let out a sigh of relief. "I'll talk to him as soon as we hang up. If he isn't there, I'll put a note on his door. Knowing his sleeping habits, I'll tell him you need to leave by 11:00. If that isn't too late for you. Unless one of us tells you otherwise, you're on for tomorrow. Thanks!"

"11:00 works for me," said Jane.

As soon as Pearl hung up, she scrawled a note she would leave for Westin if he didn't answer the door.

"C'mon, Buckley. Let's go to Westin's."

Pearl stood and Buckley leaped from the couch. They walked to Westin's shed and Pearl knocked on the door. No answer. She knocked again. Still no answer. She shoved the note between the door and doorframe and they returned to the house.

With Jane going to the auction for her, Pearl could meet with Lindy and Sarah again—assuming they were available. She got out her address book and found Sarah's number. Sarah answered on the second ring.

"Hi, Sarah. Sorry for the last-minute notice, but do you have time to meet with me and Lindy today? I wanted to see how you two feel about the search for Daisy. There's a new development. Plus, I have another idea." Pearl chewed on her lip.

"Is the new development you're going to tell us about the other stolen livestock?"

Pearl sat up straighter. "No! What do you mean?"

"I talked to Lindy earlier today and she told me Sierra heard at school that someone had stolen a couple of lambs from Joanie Stockman's farm two nights ago," said Sarah. "They were really nice ones she wanted to use for breeding this fall. And I also heard that another 4-H family had a Nigerian Dwarf buck go missing."

"Oh, my gosh. That's crazy. There has to be a connection. Did they report it to the sheriff's office?" Pearl stood and paced from the kitchen to the living room.

"I have no idea. You can talk to Lindy when we meet. Maybe she knows. Is 2:00 a good time?" said Sarah.

Pearl let out the breath she hadn't realized she'd been holding in. "Sure. We can meet at the Bigfoot Café again and have pie and coffee if you want."

"Have you asked Lindy if she can come?" asked Sarah.

"No. Will you please do that? If it works for her, I'll meet you both there. You don't need to call back unless we have to schedule another time. See you then." Pearl hung up the phone, her mind racing.

She felt energized. She refused to despair that other animals had gone missing; it meant her new plan was even more necessary.

Chapter 23

There had to be a connection between the livestock thefts. Pearl had another idea that she hadn't yet shared with anyone. She considered it brilliant and planned to work on it that morning, which meant a trip to Eugene.

She drove to Jerry's Home Improvement, where she hoped to find a driveway alarm. Her plan to catch the goat rustler required a way to detect when someone came onto her property. She wanted an alarm that would alert her not only to cars, but anyone on a bicycle, a motorcycle, or even on foot.

If she could lure the culprit to Hidden Creek Farm, she could catch him in the act and stop the thefts. She knew Dan wouldn't approve of her plan, especially after Annie's murder, but she had run out of ideas. She needed a longshot.

Jerry's carried two models of driveway alarms, but Pearl didn't want to spend her day at different hardware stores comparing prices and functions, so she selected the higher priced one and purchased it.

Later that day she walked out of Kinko's in Eugene with 25 flyers advertising goat kids for sale, using old photos of kids that were now yearlings. She knew where all the bulletin boards were located and would make sure each of them had a copy of her flyer.

Pearl did her grocery shopping, posted the flyers at Coastal, Wilco, and The Farm Store in Veneta, and drove back to Middle Pass. *I hope Westin is home tomorrow because I need to get this driveway alarm installed as soon as possible. It would be a disaster if someone tries to steal a goat before my plan is operational.*

By the time Pearl got to the Bigfoot Café that afternoon, Lindy and Sarah were already seated at a table in the back. She waved and hurried over.

"Have you ordered yet?" she asked.

"Only coffee. We wanted to wait for you before ordering any food. We already know what we want," said Sarah.

Pearl pored over the menu in front of her. "I think I'm going to have a piece of the peach pie and coffee."

They lowered their menus when they heard the now-familiar rasp of Sean's cane as he shuffled out to take their order.

"Hello, Pearl. I'm assuming you wanted coffee." He placed a green Bigfoot-embossed mug of steaming java and silverware wrapped in a napkin on the table in front of her. "There's cream and sugar on the table."

"Thank you, Sean. That's so thoughtful." Pearl smiled at him and his face brightened.

He turned his attention to Sarah and Lindy. "Have you ladies decided on what you'd like?"

"That Yeti burger sounds good to me. I'd like the coleslaw with it rather than French fries. I haven't had lunch yet and it's not my night to cook, so I think I'll splurge." Sarah laughed.

"I'm only going to have fries." Lindy removed the silverware from her napkin and placed it on the table in front of her. "I don't want to spoil my appetite. I have to make dinner for my family in a few hours."

"A piece of your fabulous peach pie for me," said Pearl. "Which of you two makes the pies?"

"Henry's the cook and baker in the family." Sean finished writing the order and headed back to the kitchen.

Pearl looked from Lindy to Sarah. "I called this meeting to figure out a path forward in the search for Daisy. I assume neither of you has had any luck, or I would have heard from you. But first, Lindy, Sarah told me someone had a Nigerian buck stolen? And Joanie Stockman's sheep? I assume you knew about that."

"Yeah, the buck went missing a couple of nights ago. Kids in school were talking about it."

"That's three goats and two sheep so far! It can't be a coincidence. Did they report it to the sheriff's office?" said Pearl.

"Three goats?" said Sarah.

"Well, one of those is just speculation at this point. I'll get to that in a minute." Pearl doodled on a notebook page. "I wanted to find out what you two think at this point so we can find an agreed-upon path forward."

"Some of the owners depend on premiums at the fairs around the state for part of their income. So this is more than just pets going missing. And in answer to your question, I know Joanie reported the theft." Lindy picked at her cuticles. "In terms of finding Daisy, I'm not sure we're gonna be able to at this point. Too much time has gone by."

Pearl flinched. "What about you, Sarah?"

"I have mixed feelings," said Sarah. "What's the new development you mentioned when you called?"

"Before I tell you, let's each share what we've accomplished. You go first, Lindy."

Lindy's shoulders sagged and she sighed. "I put flyers up in downtown Middle Pass and at all the feed stores, and as far away as Pleasant Hill and Albany. But so far no one has called. That's it for me."

"Sarah?" Pearl raised her eyebrows.

Sarah fiddled with her napkin. "I've been religiously checking Craigslist, with no luck. And Lindy and I got together and did a mailing to every 4-H family on our list."

"Oh, yeah. I forgot we did the mailing," said Lindy.

"I think we've done a great job," said Sarah, always diplomatic. "But even with that, I fear Daisy is long gone."

"You both sound discouraged," said Pearl.

Lindy opened her mouth to say something but Pearl put up her hand and continued. "I still have confidence that we'll see a break in the case. I promise to tell you my plan in a minute. But let me tell you what I've done so far. Westin and I went to the auction last week and he's there with Jane right now. I gave them some flyers and also put a few on the bulletin board. I keep checking Craigslist, but obviously with no luck. I went to Zora's farm, but I didn't find any goats that didn't belong there. That woman really tests my patience. By the way, do you know if they have a German Shepherd?"

Sarah and Lindy were blank-faced. "I haven't been to their farm and haven't seen them with a dog," said Sarah. "I know she acts superior, Pearl, but it's because she came from the wrong side of town and wants to prove that she's made it. I went to school with her."

"I haven't been to their farm either. Why?" said Lindy.

"Oh, nothing...." Pearl winced and went on. "I also went to Annie Spink's. You won't believe what happened...."

"Sorry to interrupt," said Sean. He had their food on a tray in his right hand and a cane in the left.

The women had been so engrossed in what Pearl had to say that they hadn't noticed Sean approaching with their food. He transferred the Yeti burger to the table in front of Sarah, the fries to Lindy, and the pie to Pearl.

"Anything else?" he said, smiling.

They shook their heads, too busy putting napkins on their laps and ketchup on plates.

Pearl glanced up at him. "I think we're good, Sean. Thank you."

Chapter 24

The conversation ebbed, then turned to comments about the food, while the women ate. Pearl took a bite of her peach pie. When she thought about what she had to tell the other women, she felt adrenaline flood her body and squelch her appetite. She put her fork next to the pie, dabbed at her mouth with a napkin, and scanned the café. She leaned in and spoke in a whisper.

"You probably already heard, as fast as news travels in this town, but when I went to see if Annie had stolen the goat, I found her body out in the pasture."

"Body?" Lindy gasped. She froze with a French fry in mid-air. "What happened to her?"

Sarah stared, wide-eyed. "Oh no! I read about it in the paper, but had no idea you were the one who found her body. What happened to her?"

"I went to her farm looking for Daisy, like I'd agreed to do. I didn't call her first, because I didn't want to give her a chance to hide the goat. No one answered the door when I knocked, so I went out back and checked the barn. Then I saw her on the ground out in the pasture. When I got to her, I realized she'd been dead for a while. Somebody had obviously hit her over the head. *And* I think they stole another goat.

"The neighbor said she told him someone gave her a 'Dwarf Pygmy' kid, but all the goats I saw there were adults. I first thought it might be Daisy because he said she was black and white. But if someone gave the goat to her, she couldn't have been the thief. Then again, we don't know if she made up the story for her neighbor." Pearl gestured with open hands. She looked from Sarah to Lindy. Both women looked puzzled.

"I wonder who would have given her to Annie. Did you talk to law enforcement?" Sarah took a sip of coffee.

"Of course. The first thing I did was call 9-1-1. I had to go to the sheriff's office for questioning on Thursday. When I was leaving her farm, the neighbor told me he'd heard arguing and a car driving away."

Lindy covered her face with her hands, then pulled them away. "Geez, I hope it wasn't Daisy. That poor little goat has been through so much...."

"Sorry, Lindy. It was just a thought I had. We really know nothing and I'm grasping at straws here. But something is going on with all these animals missing. At least they aren't taking them for meat, though; they're all too small." Pearl shifted in her seat.

Lindy dropped the French fry she had been about to put in her mouth. She looked sick. "Don't say that. I would never want one of our goats eaten."

Pearl put her hand on her chest. "Sorry. Some people eat their goats. I thought you'd feel better hearing it was unlikely. Do you see now why I think we need a little more time?"

Sarah closed her eyes and rubbed her forehead.

Pearl sat straighter and made eye contact with each of the women. "Okay, here's my idea. I'm going to lure the goat thief out to my farm and catch him!"

Sarah dipped a French fry in ketchup and paused while she chewed it. "How are you going to manage that?"

Lindy looked skeptical. She took a gulp of her drink.

"I'm going to install a driveway alarm, and I already put up 'goats for sale' signs to lure the thief to my farm. The alarm will alert me if they come onto my property and I'll catch them in the act." Pearl sat back in her seat with her hand on her chin, waiting for a response.

Lindy leaned toward her with a knit brow. "Not to be mean, but that sounds crazy. First of all, I don't think it'll work. And if it does, why would you want to take such a big risk?"

Pearl went rigid. She hadn't expected that reaction.

Sarah put her hand on Pearl's arm. "I agree with Lindy. Why tempt fate? Aren't you afraid the person who killed Annie will go after you?"

Pearl took another bite of her peach pie and washed it down with a drink of coffee. She let out a little laugh. "I know you guys care about me. Don't worry; I'm not trying to get murdered. If someone tries to steal one of my goats, I have Westin there, too. It'll be okay. Besides, Lindy could be right. Maybe it won't even work."

Neither of Pearl's friends seemed convinced. Instead, they looked worried. It seemed that she was so caught up in her fantasy of being a hero that she had become oblivious to the danger.

"Lindy, I'll make you a deal. If we haven't found Daisy by the middle of June, I'll let Sierra have the pick of the Mini Mancha kids I'm expecting—if there are any females. I hope she likes that breed. They'll be weaned by then," said Pearl.

Chapter 25

Pearl's sleep had been fitful ever since she confessed to Dan and Jane about what had happened to Christopher. Last night she had woken several times from jumbled dreams, feeling clammy in her sweat-drenched sheets. In one she had been riding a motorbike with Dan when a rabid dog bit him. In another Buckley got rabies and bit Westin. Each time it took her a few minutes to sort the dream from reality.

The days bled into each other, with chores and daily routine. She had no visitors. Even Jane didn't have time to take away from her gardening. No goat club meetings were scheduled until June.

Pearl sat slumped in her easy chair and felt a tear slide down her cheek. Nothing seemed to be going right—or at least that's how she felt. Dan, a growing bright spot in her life, hadn't been around lately—not even to get goat milk. After a month, the ideas Pearl, Sarah, and Lindy had come up with to find the doeling had been unfruitful, and her scheme to lure the thief to her farm also failed. *How had she ever thought that would work?*

Pearl needed some goat therapy. She moved to the front porch and sat on the bench with Buckley. She observed her growing herd browsing in the pasture. The Nigerian Dwarf kids that had been born in the spring were playing King of the Mountain on a wooden structure Westin had made. Rihanna, the bred Mini Mancha she had fallen in love with and purchased that spring, stood away from the other adult does, browsing. Pearl couldn't decide whether the earless creature was cute or ugly, but she had a calm, friendly personality.

The beautiful animals took her mind off her troubles. Her thoughts shifted to the Mini Mancha kids that were due soon. *Would Rihanna give birth to one, two or three?* She reminded herself to check the kidding kit to make sure she had everything she needed for the birth. She stood to head for the barn when Buckley perked his ears up at the muffled buzz from the house. Pearl saw a car she didn't recognize coming their way, with billowing clouds of dust following it up the gravel drive. Buckley leaped off the bench, barking. She watched a silver Lexus pull into the turnout by the barn and stop.

A lithe young woman with short, spiked, black hair climbed out. She had a pack on her back and a large, wheeled pink suitcase that she pulled from the car. The girl waved at Pearl and marched toward the house, awkwardly lugging the suitcase over the gravel. Buckley stood in the front yard, not sure what to make of her. He barked ferociously while backing toward the house.

Only when the girl got a few feet away did Pearl recognize her. It was her 16-year-old niece Scheherazade, with her hair chopped off and dyed black. She had several facial piercings that Pearl couldn't imagine her sister Ruby approving. Rather than her usual fancy designer clothes, she wore pink-and-black animal print bell bottom leggings, a black crop top, and flip-flops. Her thick black eyeliner reminded Pearl of a South American coati. *How long had it been since she had visited at the farm? Ruby hadn't said anything about her coming out.*

Scheherazade and Pearl had never been particularly close, even though her sister's family lived in Eugene. Scheherazade had uncharacteristically called a few times over the past year to vent about her mother and her life.

"I'll be darned! Scheherazade!" said Pearl.

"Scheri!" her niece corrected her, frowning. She dragged the ungainly suitcase up the steps and into the house.

Pearl was dumbfounded. "Okay. Scheri. Don't you have school this week?"

"I'll tell you once I get my stuff into the house." said Scheri. She glowed.

"Does your mother know where you are?" asked Pearl.

"No!" Scheri glowered. "Can I put my suitcase in the spare room?"

"Sure."

School didn't end for another month. *This should be interesting.* "Once you get your stuff situated, come out here and tell me what's going on."

Buckley could tell from Pearl's cheery demeanor that he shouldn't be afraid of the interloper, but he still hesitated. She didn't seem to know how to interact with him. He halfheartedly wagged his tail and followed them into the house, sniffing at the bottom of Scheri's pants but jumping back when she stopped.

"Give Buckley a little space," Pearl said. "He'll get used to you soon enough." She smiled at Scheri. "He probably doesn't remember you from the few times you visited before. Besides, you were younger."

Scheri dragged her wheeled suitcase into the bedroom. She came out sans suitcase and backpack and flopped onto the couch.

Pearl got three dog biscuits out of the pantry and handed them to Scheri. "When Buckley jumps up by me, hand him a biscuit. Then put one on your lap so he has to get closer to get it. He'll be your best friend in no time at all."

Pearl sat at the other end of the couch and Buckley jumped between them, next to Pearl. Scheri held her hand out halfway to Pearl with a biscuit perched atop it. Buckley snatched it and crunched, spitting half onto the couch while he chewed on the rest. Once he devoured the first half, he grasped the other half with his teeth and chomped. Pearl and Scheri laughed as Buckley inched closer to Scheri, not taking his eyes off the hand that held the other two biscuits.

"Don't give him the other one right away. Let him get more curious. And tell me what happened and why you're here. Not saying I'm not happy to see you...." Pearl patted Buckley's back.

Scheri shifted anxiously in her seat. "I mean. I couldn't take it anymore, Aunt Pearl. Mom wants to, like, control me, and she expects so much. She's so bougie, always worrying about her appearance. And how *I* look! It's cringe. I want to have, like, my *own* style. I think she sees me as an extension of herself, an arm or a leg. Not everything I do has something to do with her!"

"I hadn't realized you believed things were that bad. Your feelings sound pretty normal for a teenager. But your mother means well. She's overprotective because she's afraid of losing you. I'm not sure if you're aware of it, but she had many miscarriages before you were conceived, and multiple failed rounds of IVF. You're her only child and you were *so* wanted. But what happened that caused you to run away? Don't you have another month of school?"

Scheri rolled her eyes. "I took AP classes and I'm so far ahead on everything. They'll still pass me, even if I don't show up. We have the option of, like, remote classes, even though the pandemic is over. I met with each of my teachers last week, as well as the school counselor, and told them I'd be working remotely unless I needed to be physically present for a test."

Scheri held a biscuit on her palm over her lap. Buckley perked up and took it gently in his mouth and moved back to Pearl. He loudly crunched, dropping little pieces and picking them up with his lips one at a time.

Scheri giggled watching him. Then her face turned more serious. "All year Mom has been patrolling what clothes I want to wear, and, like, I'm embarrassed to be seen in the outfits she chooses. After we argued about it for a month, she threw away a college sweatshirt my ex-boyfriend gave me, claiming it was too big and looked, like, ridiculous on me. So when she left to go shopping this morning, I packed my stuff and came here."

"I'm glad that you came here rather than running off somewhere unsafe. What about your dad? What does he think?" Pearl bit her lower lip.

Scheri curled her lip. "Daddy is, like, never home. He's married to his job. Everyone thinks, like, he's so great because he gives a discount to people who can't afford braces and he works all the time, but honestly, I think he's doing it to avoid Mom and me."

"Well, you need to call your mom and tell her where you are. Do you think she'll miss you right away?"

"I doubt it. She thinks I'm in school and, like, they never bother calling parents about absences, anyway."

"I have an idea," said Pearl. "Some new people have taken over the café. Their food is pretty good and I like to patronize the local establishments. Are you hungry?"

"Sure, I could eat. What happened to the previous owners?" asked Scheri.

Pearl decided not to share all the details. "They sold the café and are living near Salem. Two men purchased it and renamed it The Bigfoot Café. They're amateur Yeti hunters. It's all decked out in Bigfoot paraphernalia. I hope things go better for them than they did for Lorena and Vern."

"Buckley, you're going to have to hold down the fort," said Pearl to her little dog, who tilted his head quizzically. She retrieved her purse and they went out the door while he sat crunching the final biscuit Scheri threw to him.

Chapter 26

Pearl and Scheri got out of the car and sauntered to the café door. Pearl yakked about how the café had changed after Vern and Lorena moved away. As Scheri reached out to grasp the handle, a thin teenager in black jeans and a dark hoody flung the door open and brushed past them in a rush. As Pearl and Scheri continued over the threshold, the screen door slammed behind them.

"Oh, no." Pearl stopped talking abruptly and put her hand to her mouth.

She whirled around, threw the screen door open, and rushed out, turning her head back and forth toward the store and the road, hoping to see the person or a vehicle. *Could it have been Zeus or the girl with him at the park?* She scanned the parking lot as Scheri stood in the doorway of the café, puzzled. Pearl couldn't see anyone. *Darn! It might have been the thief.*

Resigned, she turned back to Scheri. The roar of a car engine filled the air. She swiveled around to see a red sedan racing away on the highway.

"What was that all about?" Scheri sputtered.

"I'll tell you when we get home," Pearl whispered. "I don't want to talk about it in front of other customers. All I can say now is that it had to do with a missing goat."

They went in and sat at the far end of the counter—Pearl's normal spot when it was the Armadillo Café.

Two sets of customers were eating in the dining room area. Near the door at the counter sat Larry, Shirley, and Helen, as if nothing had changed over the past year. Pearl smiled and waved to them and they greeted her with the same.

"Solve any murders lately?" asked Helen. She talked more—and gossiped more—than the other two, unless you counted Larry pontificating about computers and other electronics.

Pearl shook her head and laughed, not wanting to reveal anything about the stolen goat.

"Who's this you've got with you?" Shirley's eyes went from Pearl to Scheri and back.

"My niece, Scheher ... Scheri. She's here for a visit. This is Shirley, Larry, and Helen."

The trio nodded and smiled. "Welcome to Middle Pass," said Shirley.

They made their way to the other end of the counter. A map marked with all the Bigfoot sightings in Oregon hung on the wall next to Pearl's stool. Below the map a numbered list detailed the locations of each sighting. Someone had highlighted the nearest ones—those in Veneta and Triangle Lake that Sean had mentioned at her last visit to the café. Pearl leaned over to read the details.

"It's a good thing I didn't see this before Pat died," she said to Scheri. "I would have suspected that a Bigfoot killed him. No offense to the dead." Their eyes locked and they burst out laughing.

"They aren't dangerous," came a male voice from the kitchen. Out popped a stocky man with bad skin who wore a blue apron with Bigfoot decorating the front. "Welcome back to the Bigfoot Café. Sean will get you menus and water in a minute. Would you like coffee?"

"Hi again, Henry. No coffee for me today," said Pearl. "This is my niece, Scheri."

"None for me either; just water," said Scheri.

Henry smiled and turned to go back into the kitchen, when Pearl spoke.

"Henry, who was the person dressed in black who just left the café?"

"I've been busy cooking back here and didn't notice anyone fitting that description." Henry shrugged and walked back into the kitchen.

A scraping sound behind Scheri and Pearl distracted them. They turned to see a tall, reedy man with thin brown hair wearing an apron that matched Henry's and clutching two menus. He moved slowly, relying on a cane to make his way across the dining room.

"This is Sean." Pearl smiled at him and reached out to take the menus.

"Hi, Sean," said Scheri.

"Welcome to the Bigfoot Cafe. I'll get your waters in a minute." Sean turned and made the slow trek past the "Do Not Feed the Sasquatch" sign to the area behind the kitchen near the water dispenser.

Pearl perused her menu and after deciding what to order, she turned to watch for Sean. Soon he reappeared, balancing two plastic glasses of water on a tray. He didn't spill a drop. He placed the tray on the yellow laminate counter between them and removed the waters, setting one in front of each of them.

Pearl turned and whispered to Sean, not wanting other customers to overhear her. "Sean, did you by any chance wait on the person in all black who left as we were coming in?"

"Funny you should ask. I don't know them. We haven't been here long enough to know a lot of the customers. But it was weird. Other than pale skin, I couldn't tell because they kept their hood up the whole time. Honestly, I couldn't tell if it was a boy or a girl. They sat at the farthest table with their back to the counter and ordered two burgers to go and paid in cash. I couldn't even tell you their eye color, because they wouldn't make eye contact. Just took the order, paid, and rushed out. Why do you ask?" Sean leaned against the wall, holding the tray in one hand and his cane in the other.

"Oh, he vaguely resembled the son of someone I know," said Pearl. She brushed her hair away from her forehead. "He sure was in a big hurry."

"Are you guys ready to order?" asked Sean.

"Not me," said Scheri. "I need a few more minutes."

Chapter 27

O nce they were settled in with salads and strawberry lemonade, Pearl turned back to the subject at hand: what had led Scheri to arrive at her doorstep and what to do about it.

"How do you think your mother's going to react when she finds out what you've done?" asked Pearl.

"I want *you* to call her," said Scheri, petulant. "I'm not ready to talk to her yet and I think she'll listen to you more than me. And I don't want to get yelled at. But is it okay if I stay with you?"

Pearl tried to hide a smile, remembering back to her younger self. She hadn't run away, but had seriously considered it in her senior year of high school. In those days there were no remote classes and no early graduation. She wasn't impulsive or brave enough to drop out, with less than a year left.

"You're welcome to stay with me, but I don't think you should go too long without talking to your parents. Still, I do think it would be a good experience for you to spend the summer on my farm. I had a similar experience that got me interested in having a farm and raising goats. I spent a summer in Nebraska on my aunt and uncle's farm." Pearl thought back to her time on the farm. "How long would you want to stay? I expect you to help out, regardless."

Scheri made a face and reached over to give Pearl a one-armed hug.

"Thank you, Aunt Pearl," she said.

"I'll call your mom when we get home. Hey, I had another idea." She looked around surreptitiously and lowered her voice. "I was going to wait till we got back home, but I'll tell you now. Someone stole a goat kid and I'm trying to find out who did it. That's why I asked about the person in black who rushed by us. I'm pretty sure it was one of two people I saw there and I wanted to ask some questions.

"Lindy, the mother of the girl whose goat was stolen and the former president of the local goat club, Sarah, and I met to talk about how to find her. The goat disappeared in March during the Skunk Cabbage Festival. We made flyers, checked Craigslist sales ads for goats in the surrounding areas, and went to the auction looking for her. I personally visited two farms on a hunch that Daisy might be there, but struck out on both counts. I'm beginning to lose faith in ever finding her." Pearl raised her eyebrows at Scheri, who eagerly listened. "We can talk later about some ideas I had."

"I'll help you," said Scheri. "It sounds like an adventure."

Chapter 28

Pearl took a deep breath and let it out slowly, trying to relax. Scheri sat on the front porch with Buckley, which would give her the privacy she needed to call Ruby. She wanted to get the conversation over with as soon as possible. She hoped it would go well, but didn't have high expectations. She and Ruby had a rocky relationship, so having her daughter run away to Pearl's farm would likely be devastating.

Ruby answered the phone after the first ring. She sounded surprised and happy that Pearl had called. She must not have discovered that Scheri left.

"Ruby, I'm calling to let you know that Scheherazade is at my farm." Pearl chewed on her lip.

"What do you mean she's at your farm? She should be in school."

"She arrived this morning, um, unexpectedly. I guess you could say she ran away from home." Pearl chuckled.

"That's ridiculous." Ruby sounded angry. "We've given her everything, so why would she do that? She's been getting more rebellious, but I didn't realize it was this bad."

"It'll be okay. At least she came to a safe place. And, anyway, the job of teenagers, beside school, is to learn how to separate from their parents. Remember when we were in high school?"

"I liked high school," Ruby raised her voice. "Even if you didn't."

"I know. But those were different times. Remember when we used to visit Uncle Hank and Aunt Vera on the farm in Nebraska? Those were some of the best experiences in my life." Pearl smiled, remembering.

Ruby scoffed. "It was okay. But what about school? She can't just drop out."

"My point was that Scheri can have the farm experience like we had, by staying here. As to school, she told me she's current with her classwork and has been able to work remotely since the pandemic. It would only be until the end of the summer. It would be a big help to me and she'll learn a lot here that she can't get in school. She has to find her wings sometime."

Ice cubes clinked as Ruby took a drink of something. *I hope she isn't drinking alcohol this early in the day.*

"I'm not thrilled with the idea, but I'm glad she didn't run off with someone who'd be a bad influence. Let me talk to Tony tonight and see what he thinks. Now put Scheherazade on the phone," Ruby ordered.

"I'm sorry, Rubes, but she's outside with Buckley. I don't think she's ready to talk right now. I think it would be a good idea for her to stay here. She could come back home for her senior year. I think having responsibilities here will help her mature."

Pearl felt optimistic that Ruby could be won over. And her husband Tony was a level head. She hoped he would agree. She had begun to like the idea of having her niece there.

"I get it!" Ruby snapped, bursting Pearl's balloon. She raised her voice. "I don't understand. She's changed so much in the past year. We always got along so well and out of nowhere she changed her name and how she dresses. She never wants to talk to me and when she does, she judges everything I say or do."

"Ruby, it's going to be okay," said Pearl, in a soothing voice. "I believe that. It's just a phase. She still loves you. You *have* given her a good life. You didn't struggle a lot as teenager, but I did, so I think I understand a little better. And remember that everything turned out fine for me. Like it will for her, too. If you need to talk more, call me anytime."

"Okay," said Ruby, sniffling. "I'm still not thrilled with the idea, but I'll call you back after I talk to Tony. And take good care of my baby."

Pearl hung up. *One of the problems is thinking of Scheri as her baby.*

Pearl walked out to the porch to tell Scheri how the call had gone when a loud cry emanated from the barn.

Chapter 29

"What was that scream?" Scheri sat upright, eyes wide.

"I think Rihanna is having her babies." Pearl went back into the house, grabbed her coveralls, and exchanged her slippers for muck boots.

"Come with me. We need to get you some coveralls and muck boots. For now your shoes will have to do."

They ran to the barn, where another loud cry echoed out. Pearl had put Rihanna in a kidding pen earlier that morning because the doe had been uncharacteristically fighting with other goats and her tail ligaments were completely softened—a sure sign that she would give birth in the next 24 hours. The kidding had begun.

The two of them walked in the side door and through the gate into the goats' sleeping area. Another cry erupted from the goat as they headed toward the kidding pen.

They got to the pen in time to see a goat, in the caul, slip out of Rihanna, who rested on her front knees. The doe twisted to reach and lick her baby, breaking the membranes. The baby thrashed, as Rihanna licked her face clean. She lay down and continued the work of cleaning off her baby.

Pearl turned toward Scheri. "See, they can do it themselves. Ninety-nine point nine percent of the time, humans don't need to intervene."

Scheri stood with her mouth open and clapped her hands. "Wow! Like, I can't believe I saw a goat being born. Do you think she has any more babies in there?"

"I suspect there's one more, but it's hard to tell. They can surprise you. There could be one, two, or none."

The kid, mostly cleaned and trying to stand, bobbed on her legs and fell forward.

"It can already stand up?" said Scheri, eyes wide.

"Yes. Because they're prey, animals like goats and deer have to get mobile as soon as possible. Not like humans."

They watched the kid try to stand again. Its legs were spread out like a hobby horse, and it swayed a little. It took a few hesitant steps toward its mother and fell again. Within seconds the kid was up again, wobbling toward Rihanna. Her licking pushed it toward the udder and after several tries, the kid finally latched on and nursed vigorously.

Scheri shook her head in disbelief.

"We'll wait another half hour to see if any more are born," said Pearl. "Then I'll go in the stall to check to see what sex they are and make sure they're nursing well. I normally bring a bucket of warm water with molasses to the mom, along with a bowl of oatmeal when she's done. It's a reward for the hard work."

Pearl laughed. "Come on, let's get started on that."

"Don't you need to be around if she has another one?" asked Scheri.

"It depends on the goat," said Pearl. She looked around at the rest of the goats, which sat chewing their cuds, seeming oblivious to what had happened.

"Rihanna isn't that trusting and she wanted to be alone. If they're disturbed or feel unsafe, they can stop their labor—another characteristic of a prey animal. We don't want that. Especially if it pushes the birth to the middle of the night.

"Other goats, like Jinx, want me there every moment, petting and reassuring them." As if on cue, Jinx walked over to Pearl and stood next to her, silently asking to be petted. "See what I mean about Jinx? She was my first goat, so she got used to lots of attention. Anyway, let's get going on Rihanna's reward."

Pearl scurried to the other side of the barn with Scheri trailing behind her. She grabbed a blue bucket and handed it to Scheri. "Here. Fill this. You can use straight hot water. They prefer it that way. There's a jar of molasses on the shelf above the sink. Pour in one fourth cup of molasses. You can guesstimate."

Pearl walked to the milking room and got a purple bowl. She filled it with some oatmeal from a jar on the shelf and walked back to the sink. Once Scheri had prepared the bucket of water, Pearl added some hot water to the bowl to wet the oatmeal.

They heard the sound that Scheri now knew came from a goat giving birth to a baby. In no hurry, they went back in and toward the stall. There lay a smaller baby, getting the same treatment as its larger sibling had gotten earlier. The first kid, mostly dry, sat next to its mother.

Pearl went in with the bowl and bucket. She hung the bucket from a hook and put the oatmeal on the divider between stalls until Rihanna completed her work. She got a film canister and iodine from the birthing kit, along with a towel to completely dry the new creatures. One by one she picked them up, rubbed them with the towel, and dipped their umbilical cords in the iodine she had poured into the film can. At the same time, she learned that both kids were females.

"Why are you doing that?" asked Scheri.

"It prevents bacteria from getting into their bloodstream." Pearl finished her task, put away the iodine and film can, and placed the bowl of oatmeal in front of Rihanna. The goat ate ravenously. Then Pearl brought over the bucket of water and watched her gulp down more than half of it.

"I think she's done," said Pearl. "Otherwise, she probably wouldn't have wanted to eat and drink. Now that the kids are both nursing, we need to leave her some alfalfa and go away to let the babies bond with their mama. We can go in the house and turn on the baby monitor, in case I'm wrong. I'll come out later to see if the placenta is out."

"When can I hold them?" asked Scheri.

"Later this evening," said Pearl.

Chapter 30

"Aunt Pearl, do you want to go into town with me today? I haven't spent any time in Middle Pass and want to check it out."

"Not really. I've seen enough of it and have a milk customer coming over this afternoon." Pearl finished washing the last dish from that morning's breakfast of pancakes and eggs and handed it to Scheri to rinse and dry. "Before you leave, do you want to go out to the barn to see the baby goats this morning? They need to be handled every day so they get used to humans."

"Sure! Have you named the babies? Can I name one?"

"No, I haven't," said Pearl. "You can name one, but I have the right to reject any names I don't like."

Pat had always begged to name the bucklings but Westin didn't seem to care. Pearl conceded most of the time because the majority of bucklings would get "wetherized," as he called it, and be sold as pets. Sarah had told her that the new owners usually wanted to name them, so whatever Pat called them wouldn't stick, anyway. Only the highest quality males got to stay bucks and be used for breeding.

The girls were a different story. They would be registered and have a full farm name, which became permanent. Pearl particularly disliked the Disney names that little girls were so fond of. She hoped Scheri didn't suggest one.

Before they could get out the door, the driveway alarm buzzed. Out the front window, Pearl saw Dan's car coming up the driveway. A smile grew on her face.

"Who's that?" Scheri stared at her, smirking. "Is that your boyfriend? Seems like it, from the look on your face."

"Just a milk customer and a friend," said Pearl. "Also, he's the sheriff."

They went out to the porch to greet him. Buckley raced down the steps and across the yard, jumping on Dan's legs.

"Looks like you aren't the only one who likes him, bro," Scheri snickered.

Pearl clenched her jaw. *Bro? Is this how she talks to Ruby?*

Dan stepped onto the porch with Buckley under one arm and an empty Ball jar in his other hand, distracting Pearl.

"Come on in," said Pearl. He followed her and Scheri into the house. "This is my niece, Scheri. She's staying here for a while."

He placed the jar on the table and put Buckley on the floor. "I'm Dan," he said, holding his hand out. They shook hands. Scheri went to the couch, followed by Buckley, and opened her book.

"I'm sorry I can't stay for long. I have to get back to the office to work on a case we're investigating." He watched Pearl at the refrigerator sorting through jars.

Finding the freshest milk, she pulled it from the refrigerator and handed it to Dan. He took the milk in one large sun-leathered hand and put his other hand gently on Pearl's arm. "Thanks," he said, with eyes twinkling.

Pearl's knees felt weak and a little shudder went down her spine. "You're welcome," she stammered. "Do you need to leave right away?"

"Sadly, I do. See you next week for more milk?" he said.

Pearl nodded and escorted him to the door.

"Are you sure he isn't your boyfriend?" said Scheri as soon as Pearl had shut the door.

Pearl felt her neck and face go red. "No. Why do you say that?"

"I saw the way he looked at you. I think he's after more than your goat milk."

"I-I don't know what you're talking about," said Pearl testily. "Now let's get out to the barn to check on those goats."

In the mud room, Pearl exchanged her slippers for her muck boots. She frowned at Scheri's sneakers. "We need to get you some farm boots if you're going to be around all summer. How many pairs of shoes did you bring?"

Scheri stared at her feet. "Only three. These, my black boots, and some sandals."

"Those will have to do for now, but be careful not to ruin them with manure."

Scheri wrinkled her nose at the thought. "Now I'm low-key paranoid."

They traipsed out to the barn with Buckley tagging along behind. "What are the best places to go in Middle Pass?" asked Scheri.

"There isn't a lot there. It depends on what you want to do. You're too young to drink, so the Middle Pass Pub is out of the question. The park is a great spot if you want to relax, watch birds, or simply enjoy nature. On the main street, there's a resale shop run by the Fluffy Fur Cat Rescue, Ace Hardware, Scraps quilting and craft shop, a barbershop/hair salon combo, The Book Nook, The Wooden Cup coffee shop, the little grocery store ... that's all I can think of at the moment. Oh, yeah. A flower shop and a bail bondsman. Hopefully you won't need that." Pearl chortled.

Scheri rolled her eyes at the last comment. "That's a good start. I like doing crafts, so I think I'll check out the craft and quilting shop."

"Do you need any money?" Pearl opened the barn door and they walked in.

"I have one of mom's credit cards and about $50 I saved because I didn't want to come here broke. Mom usually gives me money or her credit card whenever I need to buy anything."

They continued through the inside gate to the loafing area and the kidding pen. Scheri and Pearl stood in front of the gate and watched Rihanna chew her cud, cozied up to her two daughters.

"Oohh," said Scheri. "Can I go in?"

"Sure, just be calm and slow. I'm going to refill her water bucket and give her some more alfalfa."

Pearl unlatched the gate and relatched it after they were inside the pen. Rihanna didn't move. She lay there next to her kids, content.

"Will she mind if I pick one up?" Scheri crouched next to the goats.

"As long as you stay in the stall, she should be fine."

Scheri picked up the tan one with brown spots, the smaller of the two. She lifted the kid to her chest in a gentle hug. The doeling lay motionless, not bothered.

Pearl hauled the bucket out of the stall and returned shortly with clean water and an armful of leafy alfalfa that she added to the feeder. She looked at Scheri, who glowed.

"Can I name her Taylor? Her mom is Rihanna, who's a singer, and Taylor Swift is, too, so that fits. Please," she pleaded.

Pearl thought for a minute. "I can go with that. Hidden Creek Taylor Swift will be her registered name. I'll name the other one Hidden Creek Beyoncé."

"That's fire!" said Scheri.

Pearl wrinkled her forehead and stared at her niece. *That's a new expression.* She would have to google it later.

Scheri traded Taylor for the second kid. Beyoncé wasn't having it, though. She immediately screamed like she was being tortured, which caused Rihanna to stand and sniff at her. Taylor took that as a cue to rush over and start nursing. Pearl shook her head in amusement.

Scheri put the protesting kid on the straw and watched her dash to her mother, who munched on alfalfa, and latched on next to her sister.

Pearl felt a wave of sadness overcome her. "I was thinking about Sierra having her doeling stolen. I'd lose it if someone stole one of my goats."

"Yeah. That would be heartbreaking," said Scheri. She took one last look at the family group.

They let themselves out of the stall, stopping to pet the other goats that approached them. Even though Pearl named each one that came near, she knew she'd have to repeat them numerous times before Scheri remembered.

Chapter 31

Scheri got home late in the afternoon after her foray into Middle Pass. She brimmed with excitement when she rushed into the house. Buckley let out one bark and jumped on her legs. Scheri seemed oblivious to him.

"Aunt Pearl, you'll never guess what happened!"

"Save me the effort. What happened?"

"I got a job." Buckley quit trying to get their attention and retreated to his dog bed.

"In town?"

"No, Junction City. How far away is that?"

"About 25 minutes, depending on where in Junction City it is. How'd you get the job?"

"After going to the craft store and the park, I decided to, like, stop in the Wooden Cup and have a mocha. A hot guy sitting alone started talking to me. He said he needed, like, a part-time receptionist for his business. It's for six hours a day, three days a week. When I told him I was 17, he said I was old enough to do the job. He's, like, going to show me the ropes. Besides, it'll be good experience for after I graduate."

Pearl bit the inside of her lip. "So tell me more about the job and this guy. What business is it? Is it legitimate?"

"Of course it is." Scheri crossed her arms. "His name is Jeff Broadsky and he owns Pasture Pals Petting Zoo. Jeff is really nice and, like, I think it would be fun to work there. Plus it means I can pay you some rent. And I would still have time to help you since it's only part time."

Pearl thought back to her interaction with him at the Skunk Cabbage Festival. Despite initial misgivings, she figured a job would be good for Scheri. She would just have to keep a close eye on things.

She frowned. "You don't need to pay rent, sweetie. But it should be a good opportunity for you to get into the work world. What else do you know about the owner?"

"Not a lot. He told me he's, like, 26. And he started the business all by himself because he loves animals." Scheri's cheeks flushed.

"When do you start?"

"He wants me to start on Monday. I don't have to be there until like 10:00 and I'll work till 4:00 Monday, Wednesday, and Friday."

"Well, congratulations." Pearl pinched her lips together. Scheri's announcement came out of left field. It conflicted with Pearl's fantasy of them spending most days together and teaching her about farming. She went to the kitchen and pulled out her Instant Pot to start dinner.

"Is broccoli cheese soup okay with you?" she asked, pulling a bag with broccoli and two carrots from the fridge.

"Oh, I love it. And I almost forgot, I stopped in the bakery and got some artisan bread. That'll be perfect with the soup. I left it in the car. Let me run out and get it."

What will Ruby think about Scheri getting a job? Her sister could be so overprotective. She made a mental note to google Jeff Broadsky and Pasture Pals Petting Zoo so she could learn more. She wanted to be able to assure Ruby that her daughter was safe and in good hands.

Chapter 32

Pearl ran and swatted the air as a swarm of bees buzzed around her head. She jolted awake and the buzzing stopped. She sat up in her bed and looked at the clock. It was 2:30 in the morning. She remembered the driveway alarm she had installed. *Who could possibly be here in the middle of the night?*

She crept into the living room and peered at the driveway out of the break in the curtains. No headlights or car coming up the driveway. The only cars parked there were the Subaru, the Lexus, and the van. She peered down the driveway and made out a figure at the bottom of the driveway walking her direction. *I should have put an intercom in Westin's shed. It's too late now.*

A figure dressed in dark clothes hiked up the driveway and turned toward the barn's side door. *Thankfully, the moon is full.*

She rushed into the mud room, grabbed her flashlight, and pulled her coveralls on over her nightgown. She jammed her bare feet into muck boots and opened the front door.

Keeping her flashlight off, she sneaked toward the barn. She would wait outside for the person to exit. She didn't dare risk going in after him. A gun would be more of a deterrent than her flashlight, but she knew she wouldn't be able to use a firearm on anyone. As a nurse, her life's work had gone into saving lives, not taking them.

She stood outside the barn, hands shaking, for what seemed a long time while she listened to the sounds of rustling inside. *Should I go in and stop him? What if he hurts the goats?* The inside gate clicked. Moments later, the thief came out the side door, carrying one of Rihanna's kids.

"Stop!" screamed Pearl. "Westin! Come out and help me. Thief!"

The bandit glanced at her and took off toward the driveway, leaving the barn door wide open. He had only a slight head start on Pearl, who had switched into Mother Bear mode when she saw the kid in the thief's arms. The mysterious figure ran toward the highway, not gaining any ground on Pearl. His small stature and the weight of the kid worked against him. Pearl followed, closing the distance between them, as she wielded the flashlight in her right hand.

"Leave the goat, Zeus!" she shrieked.

She felt the pounding of feet and heavy panting behind her. She didn't dare turn around or she would never catch him. Only inches behind the perpetrator, she grabbed his jacket and dropped her flashlight in the process. He stumbled and the kid flew out of his arms as he let go to catch himself. The kid let out a cry, got up, and ran back toward the barn. Pearl collapsed on the thief, gasping, and tried to hold him on the ground. Despite being smaller than her, he wriggled free. Pearl crawled toward him as he got on his knees and then his feet.

Westin's voice rang out: "Stop. I have a gun."

The thief stumbled two steps when Westin closed in and tackled him. He fell forward and lay there in submission, as all three of them panted from the effort.

Pearl stood and turned toward the barn, scanning the area for the doeling. She had run that direction in terror and was leaping at the fence behind the barn in a panic to get away. Pearl rushed over and grabbed her before she could injure herself or run the other way. She held the kid, feeling the little animal's heart pounding harder than her own.

"Get up," commanded Westin.

She spun their direction and saw that Westin, barefoot and clad in plaid pajama pants and T-shirt, had the thief by both arms. He pulled the culprit to a standing position.

"Bring him into the barn," said Pearl. "I have to put this baby back." She felt a throbbing in her right knee.

She hobbled into the barn, left the door open for Westin, and turned on the light. The goats were in family groups on the sleeping shelf and floor of the barn. The thief had left open the door on the stall that held Rihanna and her other kid, but they had stayed put. Pearl gave the kid a once over to check for injuries, but she seemed fine. She took her to Rihanna and latched the stall door when she left.

She limped over, let herself out the gate, and turned her attention to Westin and the struggling bandit on the other side of the barn. Westin held him by one arm.

"Take his balaclava off," said Westin. He stood behind the thief and grabbed his other arm.

Pearl yanked on the top of the black hood and pulled the black mask off his head.

Chapter 33

Pearl and Westin gasped. A teenage girl stared at them, wide-eyed.
Pearl regained her composure. "We need to tie her up until the sheriff gets here."

She went to a shelf and grabbed some bailing twine. She held out two lengths of orange twine left from opened bales of hay. "Hold her and I'll tie her hands and feet so she can't get away. When did you get a gun?"

Westin laughed and shook his head. "Never. I just wanted to scare him ... I mean her."

Pearl tied a piece of twine around the blonde girl's wrists, which Westin held together in front of her. She crouched in front of the teen, wincing when she bent her injured knee, and knotted the twine loosely around her ankles. Pearl stood and rubbed her damaged knee.

"We're going to need some scissors when the sheriff takes her into custody because those knots are pretty tight. Watch her while I go call the sheriff's office." Adrenaline coursed through Pearl's veins like a rushing river. They had done it!

"What's wrong with your knee?" Westin furrowed his brow. "I can make the call so you don't have to walk."

"No. I can do it. I did hurt it a little when I fell trying to stop her. But I'll be okay."

Pearl hobbled to the house, gingerly climbing the front steps and entered the front door. Oddly, Buckley didn't bark.

Out of the spare bedroom came Scheri in black silk pajamas, eyes wide. She held Buckley in front of her with one arm.

"What's going on?" she asked. "I heard that buzzer and the front door closing. When Buckley started to whine at my bedroom door, I got up. I couldn't find you in the house so I looked out the window but didn't see anything."

She watched Pearl limp to the phone. "Oh, no, Aunt Pearl. Are you okay?"

"I hurt my right knee a little. But my plan worked. We finally caught the goat thief. The only thing is, it's a girl! I came in to call the sheriff's office. We tied her with baling twine in the barn and Westin is watching her."

Scheri gasped and flopped onto the couch. "A girl? What was she doing? Did she try to take a goat?"

"Yes, one of Rihanna's kids. She's too young to even be weaned and it's hard to get them to take a bottle after nursing on their mom. She might have died if the girl succeeded. But I was waiting for her." Pearl's pursed lips changed to a smirk.

She joined Scheri on the couch and dialed Dan's cell phone number. "Hi, Dan. It's Pearl. I'm sorry to bother you at this time of night, but Westin and I caught the murderer trying to steal a kid from my barn. She's tied up in the barn with Westin watching her."

He let out a big sigh. "Did you call 9-1-1?"

She looked at Scheri and rolled her eyes. "No, I didn't call 9-1-1. The last time I reported a goat theft, you guys didn't do anything, so I wanted to call you first."

Pearl paused, listening.

"You're going to be the death of me," said Dan. "I'll call the deputies myself and get over there as soon as I can. And don't do anything else until I get there."

She grimaced. "Okay, I know the drill. I'll be waiting in the barn."

She hung up and turned to Scheri. "Stay here with Buckley while I go back to the barn."

"Is it safe?" asked Scheri.

Pearl nodded. She went out the front door and shambled to the barn.

The girl sat hunched on a straw bale, staring at her hands tied in front of her, when Pearl came in the door. Westin rested on another bale, watching her.

Pearl took a seat next to Westin. "Cops are on their way."

The girl jerked her head up. Her face was ashen.

"What's your name?" asked Pearl.

"Kaylee," she whimpered.

"How'd you get here?"

Kaylee shook her head, mute.

"We know you stole at least two other goats and killed a woman in the process." Pearl felt her left knee for damage. Nothing, other than an abrasion.

The girl looked at her. Her face went from white to red. "No! What are you talking about?"

She wailed and lifted her tied hands to rub her eyes.

"No. No. No," she muttered. "They said it would be easy." It was almost a whisper.

Pearl's ears perked up. "Who?"

"No one," the girl squeaked.

Pearl continued. "We know about the other animals. And we know you were at Annie's farm," said Pearl.

The girl shook her head, not responding. Tears fell from her eyes.

The reverberation of sirens got closer, until the sound of an engine and crunching gravel told them the police had arrived.

Chapter 34

A male and a female deputy got out of the car as Pearl came through the barn door.

"You again?" said Deputy Deatherage, shaking her head. "Tell us what's going on."

"We have a girl restrained in the barn. She was trying to steal one of my goats." Pearl stood with her hands on her hips and leaned against the side of the barn to take the weight off her knee.

"Let's go in and see," said the male deputy.

They paused and turned around at the sound of a car arriving. Sheriff Dan pulled up as they entered the barn.

"What have we got here?" asked Dan, from behind them. He looked at the thin teenager sitting on a bale of alfalfa held together by three strings of orange twine identical to that securing her wrists.

"She was trying to steal one of Rihanna's new kids, but Westin and I caught her!" Pearl's heart pounded. She could hardly believe that her plan had worked.

"The driveway alarm woke me up and I rushed out to grab her. Luckily, Westin heard me yelling and stopped her after she got away from me."

The girl's chin trembled and tears trickled down her cheeks.

"What do you have to say for yourself?" Dan asked her.

She thrust her chin out and glared. "I didn't take any other goats and I didn't kill anyone."

"Then how do you know about other goats or killing someone?" Dan rubbed the back of his neck.

"They told me." She gestured with her head toward Pearl and Westin.

Dan gave Pearl and Westin a steely look.

"Why were you trying to take this goat?"

Kaylee's shoulders slumped. "I- I- don't know."

"Yes, you do," said Dan. "What were you planning to do with it?"

She closed her eyes tight and didn't respond.

Dan turned to the deputies. "Take her to the station and process her," he said. "I'll take the report from these two and be there shortly."

Deputy Deatherage turned to Westin. "Do you have scissors or a knife so I can get this baling twine off her?"

"Let me get the hoof trimmers. They'll work." He strode to the milking room and came back with orange-handled trimmers.

After he cut the baling twine from her wrists and ankles, the deputies grabbed the girl by the arms and secured handcuffs on her bound wrists. They brought her to a standing position and escorted her out of the barn to their vehicle. Once everyone was seat-belted in the vehicle the male deputy backed out and turned toward the highway.

The sheriff looked at Pearl, shaking his head. "Pearl, how is it that *your* goats were targeted for theft? You're lucky it turned out all right and you didn't get hurt."

Pearl stared at the ground. "Um, actually, I did slightly injure my right knee."

Dan furrowed his brow and leaned in closer. "Are you okay? Do you need to have it checked out?"

"No. I'll ice it and take some ibuprofen when I get back to the house."

He stared at her, blinking. "Back to the question: why your goats?"

Pearl looked sheepish. "In case you weren't aware, lots of livestock have been stolen over the last few months. But, uh, ... remember that driveway alarm I told you about? Um, I bought it to catch someone

I lured out here. I put flyers around town and in the feed stores advertising goats for sale. Apparently, Kaylee fell for it."

She glanced at Westin and covered her mouth to hide the smile coming over her face. Dan crossed his arms and a crease settled on his forehead. He seemed at a loss for words.

He pulled out a notebook and pencil from his tan shirt pocket. "Okay, tell me exactly what happened."

"I was asleep when the alarm went off. I looked out the window and saw a figure dressed in black coming up the driveway. Thank goodness we had a full moon tonight. Anyway, after I saw him ... I mean, her...go in the barn, I grabbed a flashlight and put on my boots, then snuck out. I stood by the barn, listening. A few minutes later the thief came out with a goat kid. I didn't stop to think; I just didn't want one of my new babies stolen. I yelled and she took off. I ran after her and tackled her.

"Beyonce—the goat kid—went flying onto the ground and ran back toward the barn. I screamed for Westin, who luckily is a light sleeper." Pearl looked over at Westin. "Kaylee got out from under me about the time he got outside and he yelled at her to stop because he had a gun. She froze and he recaptured her. I got the goat kid and took her back to her mom. Westin brought her into the barn and he held her while I took off her balaclava. That's when we found out it was a girl. We tied her with the baling twine and I called you."

"Any idea how she got here?"

"No. I have no idea. I didn't see a car and I don't recognize her as a local," said Pearl.

"Okay. That's probably all I need from you for now. On another note, why did you tell her about the other thefts and the murder? We have reasons for keeping some details from a suspect." A vein on his forehead pulsed.

Westin winced and looked away. Pearl felt her stomach roil.

"I'm sorry," she said, looking sheepish. "I wasn't thinking. I figured it had to be the same person and expected her to admit to it."

The sheriff turned to Westin. "Do you have anything to add?"

"No, except that I don't really have a gun. I just said that to scare her into stopping."

"That shouldn't matter anyway unless you're a felon," said Dan brusquely. He wasn't smiling.

Westin crossed his arms over his chest and glared at the sheriff. "I'm not a felon."

Okay," said Dan. "That's all."

Lips tight, he walked out the barn door to his car.

"Damn!" said Westin, glowering, as his eyes followed Dan from the barn window. They watched his tail lights recede down the driveway.

"This is bull!" Westin slammed his open hand on the barn wall. "He should be thankful we're doing their work for them."

Pearl collapsed on a straw bale. "I feel sick. I think he'll get over it, but at least we caught the culprit!"

She held up her right hand for a high five and Westin halfheartedly slapped his hand against hers. "Now, let's get back to bed. We can talk about this in the morning, although I think I have too much adrenaline in my bloodstream to sleep."

Westin nodded. He turned and walked out of the barn toward his shed. Pearl went into Rihanna's stall for one last check on her and the kids. They had calmed down and were sleeping, the two kids curled against her side.

Chapter 35

The next morning Pearl was walking on air—until her throbbing knee and battered body reminded her otherwise. While her adventure the prior night made for a good story, she realized she had probably acted rashly and remembered how mad Dan had been.

After swallowing two ibuprofen tablets with goat milk, she sat at the dining room table.

Scheri looked concerned. "Are you all right? Do you need some coffee?"

"Yes on the coffee. I'm mostly okay," said Pearl. "On the one hand, I'm thrilled that we finally caught the goat thief—but we still haven't found the stolen goats. Once they question Kaylee, I expect we'll find out."

Scheri shook her head and laughed. "I meant physically. Is your knee okay? Do you need to see a doctor?"

"No, it'll be fine. I need to stay off it for a few days, ice it, and take anti-inflammatories. I did get a few bruises I didn't notice last night and I feel like a truck hit me. But other than that ... Thanks for holding down the fort this morning. Would you be kind enough to bring me some toast with the coffee? I need something more on my stomach with these pills. Also, will you get me one of those ice packs in the freezer to put on my knee?"

"Of course. Did the girl take Taylor or Beyoncé?" Scheri jumped up and retrieved the ice pack from the freezer and took it to Pearl. She set to work pouring coffee and putting bread in the toaster.

"It was Beyoncé. I still can't get over the fact that it was a girl. That wasn't on my bingo card. I didn't even realize it wasn't a boy until we got her in the barn and took off her mask."

Pearl was solemn. "I'm nervous because Dan seemed mad about me putting myself in danger. I also made the mistake of accusing the girl of stealing other animals and killing Annie."

"Why's that a mistake?"

"Law enforcement likes to start an interview leaving out what they know so they can get the suspect to divulge more. Strategy."

"So you think she also killed that woman?"

"I'm not sure. It seems likely. I guess we'll find out what else she's guilty of once the investigation is done. What time do you have to go to work?" asked Pearl. "Are you excited about your first day?"

"I have to be there at 10:00 so I need to leave here about 9:30. I'm excited, but my anxiety is coming out."

Scheri wore baggy black jeans and a pink tank top. Pearl nodded approvingly. *Not too suggestive.* Pearl couldn't help but notice that her niece had on more makeup than usual, but decided to say nothing. *You have to pick your battles.*

Scheri brought Pearl's coffee and toast to the table, along with a small pitcher of goat milk and some plum jam that Pearl had canned the year before. Pearl poured a generous amount of milk into her coffee and took a sip.

"I understand. It's your first job, after all. But don't worry; you'll do fine. You have to make sure you can keep up with your school work though."

Scheri scoffed. "I have less than a month until school is out for the summer. I'm sure I won't have a problem."

"Okay." Pearl froze with the butter knife in her hand. *This must be how she treats Ruby.* She swallowed and spread jam on half her toast.

Chapter 36

With Scheri out working, the solitude was a nice change of pace. Pearl had forgotten how much she appreciated her alone time. She rested on the couch, snug under a teal and gray crocheted cotton blanket, Buckley at her feet, and her leg elevated on a pillow, with an icepack wrapped around her injured knee. She had walked more than she should have already, going back and forth to the barn to milk goats. She made a mental note to teach Scheri how to milk. That was the one chore she had no backup for.

Westin had come in earlier to tell her that he gave the goats hay and fresh water and threw out scratch for the chickens. He also built her a cozy fire in the woodstove, a must on this misty day. All without any prompting. He was such a gem.

With no immediate responsibilities, it would be the perfect time to catch up with everyone. The most important thing was telling Sarah and Lindy they had caught the thief. And Jane. She hadn't talked to her since before Scheri arrived.

Pearl dialed Lindy's number. She felt her heart pounding with excitement.

"Lindy? I have some fantastic news. I caught the goat thief! I mean, Westin and I did. She was arrested last night.

Unfortunately we didn't find Daisy yet."

"Remember how I told you that I was going to buy a driveway alarm and put up sales flyers to try to lure him in? Well, after nearly a month, it finally worked."

"The driveway alarm buzzed about 2:00 in the morning. When I looked out the window, I saw someone going into the barn so I grabbed my flashlight and snuck out there. When she came out of the barn with a kid, I tackled her." Pearl felt an adrenaline rush as she retold the story. "The kid went flying, but didn't get hurt. When the girl started to get away from me, I screamed for Westin, who came out and took over." Pearl pushed herself up, trying to sit straighter.

"Yeah, I was surprised it was a girl, too. Her name is Kaylee. Do you know anyone around here with that name? A teenager?"

Pearl closed her eyes as she listened to Lindy's response.

"Okay. No, I didn't get a last name. I didn't think she was from around here. We don't even know how she got here last night, since I didn't see a car."

Pearl nodded. "I'd thought for sure it was Zeus. We called the sheriff's office and they came out and arrested her. Anyway, you probably shouldn't tell Sierra yet. I think we'll find out where Daisy is soon, but don't want to get her hopes up unnecessarily. We're so close!

"I'll call when I find out more. I need to get ahold of Sarah and tell her. Maybe we can get together after I get over this knee injury." She pushed at the ice pack with her free hand, trying to adjust it.

"Yes, I hurt it tackling the girl. It isn't that bad. I'm taking it easy and icing it right now."

"Don't worry. I'll definitely keep you in the loop."

Pearl lay back on the couch with one hand on Buckley, trying to relax her mind.

She took a deep breath and called Sarah to repeat her story.

Chapter 37

Pearl heard a loud buzz from the bedroom. A few moments—and a few barks from Buckley—later, Jane came through the door with some of her famous raspberry scones in a plastic bag.

Pearl looked up from her place on the sofa. "I'm glad you could come over. What have you got there?"

Jane stopped mid-stride and stared at Pearl lying on the sofa. "Don't get up," she told Pearl. "I can take care of things. No need to play hostess if you're sick. You can explain the ice pack later."

Jane hummed as she went to work in the kitchen. She put the scones on plates, filled the electric kettle with water and turned it on, and lined up two cups on the countertop.

"Lemon-ginger tea okay? It's good for inflammation."

Pearl grinned. "Sure. It's nice to have an herbalist for a best friend."

When the kettle whistled, she filled the teacups and put them, two spoons, a jar of honey, two paper towels, and the plate of scones on a tray and brought them to the coffee table. She moved the overstuffed gray chair across from Pearl closer to the coffee table and settled into it.

"What would I do without you, Jane? I'm glad you could come over. Tell me what's been going on in your life lately. It seems like forever since we talked."

"Working on my garden, of course. I suppose Westin told you the livestock auction was a bust. On the positive side, it was a new experience—but not one I want to repeat. Those poor animals." Her eyes welled up.

"Other than that, I have some big news to share with you." Jane's face flushed with excitement.

"Probably not as sensational as yours, I'm sure." She eyeballed Pearl's leg. "But I can't wait to tell you."

"From that look on your face, it must be good news," said Pearl. "So, spill."

"I met a man and we're going on a date this weekend."

Pearl's eyes widened. "Who is it? Tell me about him. How did you meet?"

"The garden club. His name is Harvey Bell. He recently moved to the area. He's in his early 50's, a widower, he works in financial planning, and his passion is gardening. His wife died four years ago. He said he hadn't been interested in pursuing a relationship until we met. He's taking me to that new Italian restaurant in Eugene."

"That sounds almost perfect." Pearl pressed her lips into a fine line, attempting to hide her skepticism. "Is he attractive?"

"I think so. He's in pretty good shape, probably because he stays physically active. He's got a slight paunch like so many men that age, and kind of a big nose, which doesn't bother me. Brown eyes and dark hair that's graying. About five eight. He strikes me as calm and caring." Jane's eyes shone.

Pearl cleared her throat. "I hope you have better luck this time and he's a keeper." She bit her lip as she recalled the series of men who had disappointed Jane since her husband.

"Thanks. I think he might be the one." Jane had a dreamy look on her face and seemed oblivious to Pearl's lack of enthusiasm. "But that's enough about me. What's going on with you? How'd you hurt your leg?"

"You won't believe it, but Westin and I caught the goat thief/ murderer last night!" Pearl sat forward too suddenly and winced from the pain in her knee.

"Did I tell you about the driveway alarm I had Westin install? I also put up some posters advertising goat kids for sale, with the address on them. Well, in the middle of the night, the alarm went off. I got up and peeked out the window to see someone dressed in black walk up the driveway and go into my barn. I got my flashlight and crept out to catch him."

Pearl watched Jane's face go from open-mouthed to wide-eyed in alarm.

"I was able to tackle him and get the goat, but I had to yell for Westin to help me." Pearl's voice got louder as she told the story again. "Thank goodness he isn't a deep sleeper. He wrestled the little thief into the barn and we took off the mask, only to find out that it was a girl! Then we tied her up with baling twine and called the sheriff."

Jane gasped and put her hand to her mouth. "Oh my gosh, Pearl! That's terrifying! Is the goat okay? Did you have your knee examined? Do you have any other injuries?"

"Beyoncé—the kid—was freaked out, but had no physical injury that I could find. Once I got her back in with her mom, she calmed down. She seemed fine this morning. And my knee isn't too bad. This morning I felt like I had been slammed by a buck in heat, but it's just minor bruising and stuff. I think I'll be back to normal soon, with rest and regular icing.

"I think it was worth it. And everything worked out mostly fine, except for the fact that Dan is peeved because I made the mistake of accusing the girl of murder and other animal thefts. He thought it could harm their investigation. But I'm sure she did it! What's the chance that more than one person is running around stealing animals?"

Jane shook her head and suppressed a grin. She took a bite of scone and a drink of tea. "You're incorrigible."

Pearl laughed. She jumped when a pounding on the front door interrupted their conversation.

Chapter 38

The alarm hadn't gone off, so it had to be Westin. Buckley let out a yip, jumped off the couch, and followed Jane to the front door.

"It's Westin." Jane said, opening the door.

"Hi, Jane." He peered over at Pearl. "Okay if I come in?"

"Of course it is," said Pearl.

He walked through the door and Jane shut it behind him. She returned to her place with Buckley trotting behind her. Westin grabbed a wooden chair from under the dining room table and moved it to the living room. Needing no encouragement, Buckley jumped into his lap as soon as he sat down.

"Do you want a cup of tea and a scone?" asked Pearl.

"No thanks. I just got back from breakfast at the Bigfoot. How's the knee?"

She adjusted the icepack on her knee and sat up straighter. "A bit swollen, but the icepack helps. I'm trying to stay off it as much as possible. Thanks again for doing the chores. How are *you* otherwise?"

"I slept pretty well, but not enough. My left wrist aches a little. Last night seems like a dream." Westin fidgeted in his chair.

"Yeah. Thinking about it gives me a dopamine rush. We did good!"

Pearl and Westin grinned at each other, eyes gleaming.

Jane scoffed. "You two!"

"I'll take over the chores for the next couple of days," said Westin. You don't need to worry about anything except milking. Where's Scheri?"

"Who's Scheri?" asked Jane.

"Oh, yeah. I forgot I hadn't told you about her," said Pearl. "She's my niece, my sister's daughter. Her name is Scheherazade, but now she goes by Scheri. You've probably heard me mention her before. She ran away and came here. I called my sister and convinced her to let Scheri stay here for now. I thought it would do her some good to work on a farm."

"I *do* remember her. It'll be a big change for you after living alone so long. How old is she and why did she run away?"

"Typical teenage stuff. She's a junior in high school. Trying to separate from her parents. Feeling like she doesn't fit in. I have personal experience with that. Of course, Ruby doesn't understand because she was always the good, popular girl."

Pearl turned to Westin. "By the way, she got a job. The owner of the petting zoo hired her part time. It will give her some money and experience and she assures me that she'll still have time for schoolwork. That reminds me, do either of you know Jeff Broadsky? He's the owner of the petting zoo that was at the Skunk Cabbage Festival. He rubbed me the wrong way when I talked to him after Daisy was stolen. I question his motives." She bit her lip.

Westin shook his head. He hadn't been around long enough and, besides, Jeff wasn't a Middle Pass local.

"What do you mean about his motives? I've never heard of him, but you can never be too careful," said Jane. "Have you tried googling him?"

"Not yet. I worry that he might have ulterior motives for hiring her. He's almost ten years older than Scheri but she's an attractive girl who doesn't have a lot of life experience—overprotective mother and all. Investigating him is on my list of things to do while I'm trapped on this couch." Pearl let out a chuckle. "Although it's kind of nice not to have so many responsibilities."

"I gotta get going. I just wanted to check in on you, Pearl. I'm gonna let the chickens out and go into town for a while." Westin put

Buckley on the floor, stood up, and moved his chair back to its original position in the dining room. "Anything else?"

"Yes. How's your workload these days, Westin?" asked Jane. "I'm getting to a busy time in my garden and wanted to know if you'd be able to do some work for me."

"I'll have to check my calendar." Westin chortled at his joke. "How about this weekend? I want to stick around here for the next few days while Pearl is out of commission. What do you need done?"

"Moving heavy pots and rocks, planting, that kind of thing."

"Sounds good. I'll come by on Saturday."

"Thanks for checking on me, Westin," said Pearl. "We're going to need some more grain in a few days. Let's touch base tomorrow morning."

Westin nodded, and headed out the door. Buckley leaped onto the couch with Pearl, making himself comfortable on her blanket.

"I'd better get going, too. I still have some weeding and fertilizing I hope to get to this afternoon while it isn't raining," said Jane. "Will you be okay by yourself?"

Pearl nodded. Jane took the empty plates and cups into the kitchen and added them to the dishwasher. She closed the plastic bag that held the remaining scones with a twist tie and set it on the granite counter.

"I'll leave these scones for you to eat later. I have plenty more at home."

"Thanks, Jane. You're a dear. Enjoy your gardening and don't forget to tell me how your first date goes." She gave her a conspiratorial look.

Pearl waited for the buzz that told her Jane had gotten to the end of the driveway, and hobbled to her desk to get the laptop. Now would be as good a time as any to learn more about Jeff Broadsky; besides she hadn't checked her e-mail yet. She opened the computer and scanned her e-mail: obvious scams, a request from her bank to complete a survey, a Red Cross blood bank notice, but nothing personal.

She opened Google Chrome and typed "Jeff Broadsky" into the search bar. There were plenty of men named Jeff Brodsky, but only one other Jeff Broadsky—an expert on child sex trafficking. Pearl snorted. *Maybe an expert* in *child sex trafficking.* The photo didn't match.

No photo came up for the Jeff she was searching, which probably meant he wasn't on social media. *Kind of odd for someone in his mid-20s.*

Pearl had another idea. She went to the business lookup page of the Oregon Corporations Division website and typed in "Pasture Pals Petting Zoo." There it was: a for-profit corporation. She clicked on the articles of incorporation link. Jeff was listed as the registered agent, but the company had been around since 2005 so there was no way he started it. He would have been a child. Pearl pursed her lips in disapproval.

She clicked on the link to the initial filing for the corporation. There it was: James Broadsky, registered agent. Jeff's name was nowhere to be found.

She continued her search, googling James Broadsky. She found an obituary for Fred L. Broadsky. She read, "He is survived by two sons, James Broadsky (Ellen) and Elliot Broadsky (Sharon), two granddaughters, Sharon Kay Broadsky and Serena Lewis (Charles), and one grandson (Jeff Broadsky). So either Jeff's dad or uncle had initially incorporated Pasture Pals. *Jeff was no doubt lying to impress Scheri.*

Pearl snapped the laptop shut. *It's nothing to worry about. Plenty of people try to make themselves sound more successful than they are. At least he's providing a job for Scheri. It will be good in the long run, teaching her responsibility.*

Still, a distressing feeling nagged at her.

Chapter 39

Pearl had taken another pain pill and changed the ice on her knee when the phone rang. She sat up and reached for the receiver, grimacing from the pain.

"Hi, Pearl. It's Dan. What are you doing this weekend?"

"The usual. I expect my knee to be almost normal by then." Pearl rearranged herself on the couch, accidentally knocking Buckley to the carpet. He bounced back up.

"That's good news. I want to come by on Saturday for a while. To talk and to get some milk."

"What time?"

"Are you up by 9:00?"

Pearl burst out laughing. "This is a farm, Dan. I'm normally up with the sun."

"Okay. I thought I should ask. I'm an early bird, too. Let's plan on that. I'll even bring some donuts or sweet rolls if you supply the coffee. I'll see you then."

"Wait!" said Pearl. "Aren't you going to update me on the goat thief?"

Dan took a deep breath and exhaled. "I can't discuss that over the phone. I'll update you when I see you Saturday. I have work to do now so I need to go."

He hung up abruptly. Pearl felt a prickling sensation on the back of her neck. *The guy is hard to figure out: was he annoyed with her question or just in a hurry?*

She leaned back on the couch, mesmerized by the echo of raindrops pelting down on the metal roof. Her meditation was interrupted when Scheri flew through the door. Pearl hadn't heard the driveway alarm going off. How could it already be 4:30?

Scheri had a huge grin on her face and carried two white cartons. "Hi, Aunt Pearl. I mean, I low-key love my job! Jeff took me out for lunch at the Chinese restaurant in Junction City. Like, he even let me take the leftovers."

Pearl gritted her teeth. *Calm down, it's only a lunch.* She swallowed and pasted a smile on her face. "That's nice. How was the work? Did everything go well?"

"I'm still learning, but I'm responsible for answering the phone, scheduling events, typing things up, and, like, tracking supplies and animal feed." Scheri put the cartons in the fridge and plopped into the chair across from Pearl. "Hey, we should go to one of the events they're working sometime."

Pearl shifted her body on the couch, trying to get comfortable. "That sounds fun. Did you have enough work to keep you busy?"

"Not today. That's why we had time to take a long lunch."

Pearl frowned. "Will you get to interact with any of the animals? Like feeding them or that kind of thing? I think that would be the most fun part of the job."

"No. They aren't kept at the office. They're on a property out in Lebanon. Like, I'm not even sure where that is." Scheri pulled the goat-patterned pillow out from under her back and clutched it in front of her stomach.

"Oh, okay. How many other people do you work with?"

"It's basically, like, a two-person office. Jeff hired me because he needed a little extra help with the paperwork and scheduling. Most everything is done online or over the phone." She tapped her foot, then jumped up. "Anyway, I have to get on my laptop and catch up with school work."

"You should think about calling your parents to tell them about your job."

Scheri flipped her hair and retreated to her bedroom without a word.

"You need to think about it." Pearl yelled toward the bedroom. "And I was hoping you'd fix dinner tonight."

Scheri appeared at the threshold. "If you want, we can have the leftover Chinese." She raised her eyebrows.

"Sounds great, as long as you don't mind eating the same thing twice in a day. Let's eat at 6:00. I hope that's enough time to get your school work done."

Chapter 40

Pearl had taken the wet clothes out of the washing machine that Saturday morning and was aggravated to find that Scheri had left her clothes in the dryer. She gathered the clothes from the dryer and dumped them in a pile on Scheri's unmade bed.

I guess I should cut her some slack since it was the first time in her life she'd done laundry. She even had to be instructed on how to operate the washer and dryer.

"I put your dry clothes on the bed. You need to fold and put them away, and make your bed." Scheri sat in the overstuffed chair paging through a fashion magazine, not bothering to respond.

After two knocks on the door and two barks from Buckley, Pearl hurried through the living room, forgetting that she still needed to take care with her knee. Her cheeks glowed.

"Come on in," she said to Dan, with her arm outstretched to guide him. He carried a white bakery bag in one hand and an empty milk jar in the other. His eyes sparkled when he looked at Pearl. Buckley danced over to him, eager for attention.

Scheri placed the magazine on the couch and, with a sullen look, stared from Pearl to Dan.

"Scheri, would you mind going out to the barn and hanging out with the goats while you read? Those new kids need a lot of handling so they'll be tame when I sell them. If you get some peanuts out of the jar in the milk room, you can tempt the adults. I don't think those kids are old enough to understand that they're good to eat, although if you aren't careful they might try to eat your magazine. You can take care of the clothes on your bed when you get back."

"It's cold outside." Scheri complained as she wrapped her arms around her exposed abdomen. "I won't bother you guys."

"Maybe if you wore more clothes you wouldn't be chilly." Pearl stared at the crop top and skort she wore and chuckled. "And you *would* bother us. We're going to be talking business. Put on my insulated coveralls, if you want."

Scheri stomped to the mud room to put on coveralls and muck boots, smirking at Dan as she passed him.

Dan put the bakery bag on the table and took a seat. Pearl walked over and shut Scheri's bedroom door. She went to the kitchen and poured coffee for both of them, bringing the steaming cups and empty plates to the table where Dan sat, along with a small pitcher of goat milk.

"Not all peaches and cream, is she?" he said. "I got some almond bear claws. I hope you like them."

"Who doesn't?" said Pearl. *Dan must prefer chunky women.* Bear claws were a treat she rarely allowed herself to have. She helped herself to one of the pastries, got a knife, and cut it into two pieces.

The mud room door swung open. "I want a bear claw," said Scheri, frowning.

"You can have one when you get back. Now go!" said Pearl.

Scheri shut the door behind her.

Pearl licked her lips in anticipation. "Do you want a whole one or half? I can only eat half at one sitting."

"A whole one," said Dan. Pearl put the other half of her bear claw back in the bag and passed it to Dan. He added one to his plate.

"Your knee better? I see you don't have a noticeable limp anymore."

Pearl nodded. They sat silently, sipping their coffee until the porch door slammed.

Pearl leaned forward in her chair. "She went to work for Jeff Broadsky at the petting zoo this week. I don't totally trust her boss."

"Why's that?" Dan furrowed his brow.

"I'm suspicious that he had an ulterior motive for hiring her. She's a cute girl, but too young for him. I also did a little searching online and found out that he lied to her about being the one who started the zoo. It turns out that he took it over from his uncle or father."

Dan chuckled. "You have a suspicious nature, Pearl."

"And I'm usually proved right. Anyway, I'm keeping a close eye on things. My sister would never forgive me if Scheri got romantically involved with someone that old."

"I haven't met the man. What makes you think it's not just an employer-employee situation?"

"I sense that he has a huge ego. He's 26 and she's only 17. You know how some of these guys can be, especially the immature ones. And, like I said, Scheri is an attractive girl. She seems a bit starry-eyed when she talks about him."

"I get it. She's lucky to have you for an aunt."

Pearl smiled at the compliment. "Now to a different subject. Tell me what happened with Kaylee."

"She bonded out yesterday."

Pearl scoffed. "What? A serial livestock thief and murderer can bond out that fast? What was her bail?"

He dropped his pastry on the plate. "$25,000. And we don't have any evidence that she was responsible for anything but trying to steal your goat."

"Seriously? Did you even interview her?" Pearl's eyes flashed with anger. "And did you get a report on stolen sheep and another goat earlier? It seems coincidental that different people would be stealing livestock around the same time. Or is that common in Lane County?"

Dan touched her arm and Pearl calmed down almost immediately. "No, it isn't common. They could be connected, but you know how the system works. She invoked her right to remain silent and we need more evidence to charge her. And charging decisions are made by the DA, not me."

Pearl sighed. "Did she say anything?"

"Other than denying any knowledge of Daisy and the incident at the Spink Farm, no. After that she refused to talk. It seems obvious to me that she's protecting someone."

"I agree. Before you got here that night, she said something like 'they' said it would be easy."

"Don't worry; we aren't done with Kaylee yet. We had to let her out of jail because someone paid the bail. I think when push comes to shove and she's faced with a huge fine or jail time, she might be more forthcoming. But she has no prior record and the arrest was for a minor crime. We do have another lead, though."

Pearl shook her head and shuddered. She was so sure she had solved the crimes when she and Westin caught Kaylee. What would she tell Lindy now?

"Tell me about the lead."

Dan sighed and shook his head. "Sorry, it's confidential. And it's a lead, not evidence. Maybe I shouldn't have mentioned it."

Her shoulders drooped and she rubbed at a spot on the table, avoiding Dan's eyes.

Dan pulled his eyebrows into a deep crease. He reached across the table and squeezed Pearl's shoulder. "Don't give up yet."

"Hey, I haven't met any of your goats yet," said Dan, changing the subject. "Why don't we go out to the barn after we finish our coffee so I can see these new kids?"

Goat talk was music to Pearl's ears. "That's a good idea. It'll make me feel better. And you're going to *love* Beyoncé and Taylor."

"That's what you named them?" Dan laughed.

Pearl emptied her coffee cup and stood up. She carried the dishes to the sink and got a dishcloth to wipe the table. "Scheri wanted Taylor, after Taylor Swift, so I figured Beyoncé would be good name for the sister. After all, their mother is named Rihanna."

Dan laughed. "I didn't know people even named their goats until I met you."

They made their way to the barn, where they found Scheri sitting on the sleeping bench with Taylor in her lap and Beyoncé pawing at her arm. She appeared to be meditating.

They went through the gate and were greeted by the adult does. Pearl scratched Jinx's neck. The bucks stared from the other side of the barn.

"Why are some of the goats kept on the other side of the barn?" said Dan.

"Oh, those are the bucks. Some people run them together, but I like to control the breeding. Plus, those guys smell pretty bad for a good part of the year and I don't want to risk having the odor get into my milk." Pearl wrinkled her nose.

"The guy with the long beard is pretty handsome. What's his name?"

"Winchester," said Pearl.

"Why the gun name?"

"His sire was Remington, so they were keeping with the gun theme. I bought him from another farm."

Pearl went over to Scheri and picked up Beyoncé. "You want to hold one?"

Dan grinned and walked over with his arms outstretched. Pearl place the kid into his arms and he pulled her up to his chest. She squirmed for a minute, then settled in.

Pearl went to work dumping out water and refreshing the buckets, while Scheri and Dan sat on the bench with the kids. Both doelings were soon fast asleep.

Pearl was refreshing the hay when Dan said, "I need to get going." He placed the kid on the bench. She did a little sideways leap and ran to her mother, nursing for about 15 seconds before Rihanna walked away.

Taylor joined them and both nursed for another few seconds before their mother pulled away.

Dan and Pearl walked to the house together and made the milk transaction.

"How about a hug?" said Dan.

Pearl's heart leaped. "Sure."

He put his arms around her and she melted into him. "I know you're disappointed about the pace of the investigation, Pearl. I'll keep you informed as best I can."

They separated. Pearl could hardly believe this was happening. Dan stepped back and took her hands. "We need to set a definite date for dinner."

Pearl nodded weakly. "Okay." She felt her disappointment receding as she contemplated her first date in years.

"Let me check my calendar when I get back to work and figure out a time that works for both of us."

Chapter 41

When Sunday rolled around, Pearl admitted she couldn't put off telling Sarah and Lindy that finding Daisy was unlikely. She called and asked them to meet her at the Bigfoot Café.

That afternoon they sat drinking coffee and eating berry pie at what had become their usual table. The tables now sported cotton coverings with a brown-and-blue bigfoot and tree pattern. Sarah and Lindy looked expectantly to Pearl, whose glum expression should have signaled to them that the news wasn't good.

"You don't seem too happy, Pearl. Tell us what's up," said Sarah.

"Kaylee, the girl who tried to steal my goat, Beyonce, already got out of jail! I'd hoped that when Dan came over yesterday he'd tell me they found Daisy. Although I suppose they would have called you with the news first, Lindy." Pearl's shoulders sagged. "I've disappointed you."

Her mind flashed back to that first meeting at the Bigfoot Café and all their plans. *What a fool I've been.*

She let out a deep sigh. "I'm not sure where to go from here."

Sarah put her hand on Pearl's arm. "You've already done so much, Pearl. I think you've gone above and beyond."

"Come on, Pearl. You'd have to be superwoman to have cracked this case. And I don't see a cape," said Lindy, in an attempt to lighten her mood.

"I think we both appreciate how hard you tried, Pearl." Sarah turned to Lindy, who nodded. "Now you need to focus on your farm and your niece." She rubbed Pearl's back.

Pearl took a deep breath. "Anyway, I think it's time to have Sierra over to pick out the kid she wants, Lindy."

"Oh, Pearl, you don't have to do that," said Lindy.

"I said I would and I want to follow through with that promise. I only need so many goats anyway and it will save me having to sell to a stranger."

"That's so generous!" said Lindy. "How about the end of June. Obviously, you can't separate them from their mom at this point. You're dam-raising, not bottle feeding, right?"

"That's right. I know how hard it is to get them to take a bottle if you don't start right away. June would be ideal."

Chapter 42

That Monday, Scheri got home from her job in the late afternoon. She walked through the doorway past Pearl to the sound of Buckley's barking, and snapped at him, "Buckley, no!"

Buckley froze.

Scheri flopped into the overstuffed chair and let out a heavy sigh. Not to be deterred by a reprimand, Buckley jumped onto her lap. Scheri glared at him, but didn't make a move to get him off of her.

"What's going on?" asked Pearl. "Did something happen at work?"

"I'm overwhelmed at the amount of calls I had to take today. We're going into the busy season and apparently everyone decided to call at the same time. And, like, people can be so rude sometimes."

Pearl laughed to herself. *The child is realizing that being an adult and working is not just fun and games.*

"What happened? Who was rude?"

"I was on my own today for, like, most of the day because Jeff was out doing some other business. This lady was yelling at me because I didn't know, like, every detail about the animals. I tried to tell her I was new to the job, but she kept at it. Jeff is adding new animals all the time so he can, like, expand his business, and I can't keep up. I didn't want to hang up because she was a customer so I had, like, no choice but to take the abuse and act friendly. Finally I told her I'd have Jeff call her back."

"Oh, honey, I'm sorry you had to deal with that. Some people go through life angry and blame everyone but themselves. Hopefully you won't have too many of those. Do you have any school work to do?"

"No." Scheri picked at one of her cuticles.

"I have an idea. Since it's nice out today, let's take the goats for a hike in the woods. That'll cheer you up and you can see the route we take, so you can go out on your own sometime."

Scheri, sitting slumped in the chair, nodded. "Let me change into my jeans and a long-sleeved shirt."

She pushed Buckley off her lap and went into the bedroom. She came out after a few minutes wearing blue jeans and a yellow-and-red striped long-sleeved T-shirt. "I'll be glad to get my first paycheck on Friday so I can buy some new clothes without having to charge them on mom's card."

Buckley tilted his head at Scheri and Pearl, as though trying to determine if they were going somewhere. He didn't like being left at home alone.

Pearl got up from the couch. "Yes, you're going," she said, looking down at Buckley. He wagged his tail and repeatedly leaped in the air.

"DO YOU WANT TO LEAD or follow?" asked Pearl. They were walking toward the path into the woods behind the house.

"After Buckley, that is. He always leads, but we need someone in front of the herd and someone behind. The kids haven't been out here before, so they might get scared and run. I hope my herd never gets too big to take everyone out."

"I'll take up the rear and you can lead since you know which way to go. Do you ever take the bucks out?"

"Not as often as the does, but sometimes I do in the summer. I've tried in the fall and winter, but all they can think of is getting to the girls. They have one-track minds when they're in rut, and they're not thinking about hiking." Pearl passed the herd and headed for the path.

They trudged along the trail, stopping to admire the pinkish-white trillium and tiny flowers rising from the moss and fir needles on the forest floor. When they got to the Big Log, a mammoth tree that had fallen over the creek many years before, they rested on two nearby stumps.

"Stay away from that little log," said Pearl. She pointed to a section of tree resting on its side under the bottom left side of the Big Log. I hope they're gone now, but one time I sat on it and a swarm of yellowjackets flew out and stung me."

The goats had no interest in staying still. They went around to the other side of the Big Log, where they could climb it and cross over the creek.

"Will you go with them across the log?" said Pearl. "The kids might need some help getting up."

Scheri smiled and bounded over. Some of the does had already gotten up and were making their way across the gigantic moss-covered log. Scheri helped up two kids and followed the herd to the other side where they browsed on salal, fir branches, wild rose, and other tasty plants.

"Don't go too far," said Pearl. She sat on the stump with Buckley on her lap. The sun had made its slow descent to the tops of the hills of the Coast Range, casting long shadows over the forest. She peered up at the log and across the creek but Scheri and goats were no longer in sight.

"Everything okay? Pearl yelled.

"Yes," came a reply from the other side.

Twenty minutes later, the goats returned across the log, with Scheri behind them. Buckley jumped from Pearl's lap and led the way back to the farm, with Pearl, the goats, and Scheri following. When they got close to home, Pearl gradually let the herd pass her until she was even with Scheri.

"Better now?" said Pearl.

Scheri beamed. "I'm starting to see how goats are good for the mood, like you said."

"I'm glad to hear that. How are you liking life here otherwise?"

"Pretty well. I like having the freedom to do what I want most of the time. And not having anyone, like, judging me and criticizing my clothes."

"Speaking of that, you've been here almost two months. I think it's past time for you to call your family. Your mother has been sending me e-mails asking about you and I think you should tell her yourself."

Scheri rolled her eyes. "You're right, I guess. I haven't bothered to read the e-mails she sent me. Is she, like, freaking out?"

"I don't think it's risen to the level of freaking out, but her feelings are hurt. I hope you two can reach some kind of understanding and start talking again. What do you think about having her out to visit us?"

"Let me talk to her first before I answer that question." They walked the rest of the way in silence, shooing kids that went off the path.

"I left the gate open and they know to go in there when we get back, so we need to make sure everyone gets that far." They herded errant goats back to the path.

They watched the herd go through the gate. Scheri rushed to latch it while Buckley veered out of the way. Pearl stood back, hands on her hips, looking at the sliver of sun that showed above the hill.

Chapter 43

"Why don't you give your parents a call while I get dinner ready?" Pearl poured kibble into Buckley's bowl.

Scheri gave her a pained look. "All right. I suppose it's time."

It seemed to Pearl that Scheri had been avoiding making a call. She wanted to help mediate the situation, so Scheri could return home in the fall on good terms with her parents, not just provide a place to escape and evade them.

Pearl scurried around in the kitchen, chopping onions and slicing mushrooms for mushroom stroganoff. It was one of her favorite Instant Pot recipes and easy, too. Scheri's voice rose and fell in the bedroom where she had sequestered herself for the phone call, but Pearl couldn't make out the words.

Pearl had been talking to Ruby every week or so since Scheri arrived—keeping her informed about what her only daughter was up to and how she was doing. Her sister still acted prickly about the idea of Scheri living with Pearl. Whether or not her brother-in-law felt the same was an unknown, because they rarely discussed him. At least he had initially agreed that Scheri could stay.

Ruby sounded lonely. She had put all her energy into her daughter for years, so with Scheri gone and her husband focused on work, she seemed lost. Pearl had suggested counseling a few weeks earlier—the wrong thing to say to Ruby. It didn't fit with the perfect life she wanted to project. *Had she even told any of her friends that Scheri left?*

Pearl secured the lid on the pressure cooker as Scheri came out of the bedroom. Her cheeks were red and her lips were pinched tightly.

Pearl pushed the pressure cook button and set the timer. "How did it go?" she asked.

Scheri reached down and picked up Buckley before she sat on the couch. "I don't want to talk about it right now. I need some time to process."

Scheri held Buckley tight, burying her fingers in his fluffy fur. Buckley tried to lick her face, but she pulled him away, laughing. "No face-licking, you little punk."

"I have to make a salad, and the mushroom stroganoff will be ready in about 20 minutes. Why don't you go wash your hands and set the table?"

Without a word, Scheri stood up, placed Buckley on the couch, and went into the bathroom.

She came out smelling of almond from the liquid soap. "I'm a little worried about Mom," she said as she took two plates and two salad bowls from the cupboard. She carried them to the table and set one of each in them in their usual places.

Pearl nodded but said nothing, not wanting to push her out of her comfort zone. She pulled salad greens, avocado, and sesame salad dressing from the fridge and a flowered ceramic serving bowl from the cupboard. She opened a cupboard under the counter and removed a wooden cutting board. After retrieving a knife from the magnet on the wall, she took a tomato from a bowl on the counter and cut it into sections.

Scheri returned to the kitchen, opened the silverware drawer and took out two forks. She pulled open the drawer next to it and chose two yellow cloth napkins. She took them to the table, arranging them next to each plate.

"Do you want water?" asked Pearl.

"Yes, thanks." Scheri took two clear glasses from the cupboard and filled each with water from the filtered pitcher in the refrigerator. She set each one above the plates.

"Why are you worried about her?" asked Pearl.

"She doesn't have much of a life. I don't think she, like, has any friends she can talk to. They all seem so fake—which is something I wanted to get away from when I left home. I thought she was happy with things that way, but after talking to her tonight, I'm not so sure. What can we do to help her?" Scheri sat at the table and wrapped her arms across her chest.

Pearl stopped making the salad and turned to Scheri. "I had the same impression as you about her loneliness. What do you think about inviting her out for lunch one of these days?"

Scheri massaged her neck, looking pensive. She lifted her head and gazed at Pearl. "Yeah, I guess I'm ready for that. But, like, we need to tell her to wear casual clothes and leave the heels at home." They snickered.

Pearl finished cutting the avocado, rinsed off the knife, and put the skin and pit in the compost bucket. "How about Thursday, if that isn't too soon for her?"

She added the avocado to the lettuce and tomato mixture and carried the bowl of salad and bottle of salad dressing to the table.

"Okay," said Scheri. "Before I change my mind, I'll call and invite her after we eat. We also need to figure out what to make."

Chapter 44

Scheri's mood had improved by the time she got home from work Wednesday afternoon.

"I take it you had a better time at work today?"

"I guess Monday is, like, the worst day for phone calls. I didn't have nearly as many today, so I had time to do some filing. Jeff and I talked about me, like, designing a flyer to market the petting zoo." She stood up straight, eyes gleaming.

"I'm glad I struggled through learning InDesign; it's going to come in handy." She played with her hair. "He's a photographer, too, so he'll take all the photos. He wants to expand to senior centers, schools, birthday parties, and other venues. I think we're gonna, like, get a couple of ponies so we can do pony rides, too. It's so exciting!"

"Well ... that sounds nice," said Pearl. "Where does he get the animals for the zoo?" She raised an eyebrow, but Scheri wasn't paying attention. The question hung in the air, as she sat dreamy-eyed, off in her own world.

The spell broke and, without answering, Scheri jumped up and grabbed her in a big hug, throwing Pearl a little off balance.

"Where did that come from?" Pearl sputtered.

"I'm so happy right now. Things are going well on my job, school is almost out, and, like, I love living here with you." Scheri let go and stepped back, almost catching Buckley under her foot. Feeling the excitement, he zoomed into the kitchen, back into the living room, running a circle around a chair from room to room.

Pearl and Scheri had to sit down because they were laughing so hard. Buckley flew into Scheri's lap almost before she sat down.

"Yikes! I've never seen him like that," she said, clutching him in her arms.

"The older he gets the less often he does it. But he's still a puppy at heart."

"Oh, yeah! I almost forgot to tell you. Jeff's going to show me, like, where the animals live. We're meeting at the office and driving there on Thursday evening." She grinned broadly.

Pearl raised her eyebrows. "I hadn't realized you liked animals so much."

"Why do you say that?" asked Scheri.

"Well, you never had any pets, and until you came out here, you didn't seem interested in the goats or chickens ... or even Buckley."

Buckley tilted his head at the mention of his name.

"I *love* Buckley," Scheri said.

He gave her hand a lick and she jerked it away. "Well ... except for the licking."

She opened her mouth to say more and stopped, as if lost in her thoughts. She stared at her hands, mute.

"You know, Aunt Pearl, I didn't even know I liked animals before I came here. Like, Mom would never let me have any; she thought they were dirty. And Daddy always deferred to her."

"Whenever we came to your farm, Mom spent, like, half the drive talking about being afraid she'd get her clothes dirty and hoping you wouldn't, like, try to get her to go out to the barn where the goats would jump up on her. I was just a kid. Like, I hadn't been around animals before and I was a little scared of them. She made it sound awful and as if she was doing you a big favor to visit."

Pearl nodded slowly. She put her hand on her forehead and sat silent.

Scheri covered her mouth and let out a gasp. "I'm sorry. I didn't mean to hurt your feelings."

"No, honey, it's okay. I think you've already heard that your mother and I don't have the best history. We chose different paths in life. I hope you can see that there isn't necessarily anything wrong with one or the other; they're just different. Maybe your change of mind can help her see that, too, although it may be too much to think she'll run out and get a cat or a dog." Pearl shook her head and laughed at the thought.

Scheri nodded solemnly.

"So what time are you going to Lebanon tomorrow?"

"Around, like, 7:00. I'm going to meet Jeff in Junction City and we'll drive to Lebanon together. He's meeting someone there."

"You'll have to let me know what animals they have." Pearl decided to let her question about where they got the animals slide for now. "On another note, are you ready to see your mom tomorrow?"

"I have mixed feelings. How about you? Are you ready?" Scheri teased.

Pearl laughed. "I grew up with her, so I'm familiar with how she is and I'm always ready. I've learned how to keep my hackles down. Anyway, it'll be a nice change to have her out."

Chapter 45

Scheri and Pearl bustled around the house trying to get it into picture-perfect condition for Ruby's visit. As Scheri vacuumed the carpet, a fluffy, shiny white Buckley retreated to Pearl's bed for safety.

Scheri had insisted on giving Buckley a bath the night before. She told Pearl that she knew her mom didn't like dogs, but figured that she wouldn't be as squeamish if he seemed clean and smelled good.

"If only he can restrain himself from jumping up on her," Pearl had said.

The odor of fresh-baked sourdough bread filled the room. Pearl had prepared the baguette dough the day before and their second rise finished earlier that morning. The loaves had come out of the oven and were cooling on a wire rack.

The two of them had decided on a simple lunch of soup and bread. Pearl's recipe for broccoli cheese soup made in the Instant Pot seemed like the easiest and quickest thing. The chocolate mousse Scheri had made the previous night chilled in the fridge.

Pearl glanced out the window for the tenth time, not emotionally ready for Ruby to arrive. She saw the chickens pecking and scratching on the porch and raced out the door to shoo them away before they made a mess that Ruby would have to walk through. Sure enough; they had. Pearl threw up her hands. She went back into the house and grabbed a rag that she wet and took out to clean the mess.

Scheri had finished the vacuuming and checked the list she had made to see what they missed. "What was that all about?" she asked.

"Darn chickens pooping on the porch. Almost as though they're conspiring against your mother."

Pearl finished scrubbing the front porch when Ruby drove up in her silver Mercedes-Benz. She would no doubt be stressing out over the dust that had begun to coat her car as she motored up the driveway. Hearing the buzzing of the alarm, Scheri came out to greet her, holding Buckley.

"I want to prevent him from jumping up on Mom." Scheri tousled the white fluff on his head. Buckley whined and squirmed in her arms when he saw Ruby approaching the steps, but Scheri held tight.

"Welcome, Ruby!" said Pearl as Ruby climbed the steps. She and Scheri exchanged glances, relieved to see her in tan slacks, a pink cotton blouse, a light jacket, and canvas sneakers rather than the usual "good" clothing she normally wore. While not exactly farm clothes, they were more appropriate to the occasion. Even her jewelry was subdued, with her wedding ring, a gold necklace, and a bejeweled brooch on her shirt. Pearl doubted that Ruby had worn a T-shirt or jeans since her college days.

"We're so glad you could come out." Pearl gave Ruby a hug, while she ticked off a list in her head, fearing they had missed something in their preparations.

Scheri hesitated, then inched toward her mother. Ruby smiled at her, and shuddered at the sight of Buckley in her arms. Scheri, long accustomed to complying with her mother's desires, scowled and handed the Pomeranian to Pearl.

Ruby threw her arms around her daughter. "I've missed you so much, honey." She held on until Scheri pulled away. Ruby held her at arms' length and checked her out, a smile flickering on her lips.

"You're looking healthy," she said.

Scheri's eyes lit up with pleasure at the unexpected compliment. She had skipped her normal crop top that day at Pearl's suggestion. She tilted her head and tried to read her mother's face. "Really?" she said.

"Come on in. Lunch should be ready shortly, but we can sit and chat until then," Pearl held the front door open and gestured indoors.

Scheri led the way, Ruby followed, and Pearl took up the rear with Buckley, who stretched his neck out and sniffed the perfumed stranger.

Scheri led her mother to the couch and patted the left side before sitting on the other end. Pearl planted herself in the overstuffed chair opposite the sofa and Buckley arranged himself on her lap. Pearl hoped to avoid him jumping on Ruby by keeping him contained until everyone had relaxed.

"How's school going?" Ruby blinked her eyes at Scheri.

"Fine. I was so far ahead when I left that it's been, like, simple to keep up. I'm so glad there's only two weeks left." Scheri kicked off her slippers and repositioned her back against the arm of the couch facing her mother. She bent her knees and pulled her feet up onto the couch.

Ruby looked nervously at Pearl, who was oblivious. She bit her lip and turned to Scheri again.

"Don't you miss your friends?"

Scheri stiffened. "No. I told you I didn't have any, like, real friends."

Ruby pursed her lips and shook her head. "You're exaggerating. What about Jenny?"

Pearl rubbed Buckley's neck and watched the two of them. She thought it better to stay out of the conversation for now.

Scheri let out a sigh and crossed her arms over her chest. "Not what I would call a friend when she steals your boyfriend. Besides, she's too phony and emo."

Ruby scoffed and brushed a dog hair off her slacks. "I didn't think you were that interested in Conner. Besides, you don't want to get stuck in a high school romance. They're meant to be temporary." She jutted her chin out, a look of superiority on her face.

Scheri scowled. "Like, you're missing the point as usual, Mom. It's about loyalty. And you're right. I didn't, like, care that much about him. He had no rizz whatsoever." She shook her head and rolled her eyes.

Ruby glanced at Pearl as a deep red crept over her face and neck. She reached for her purse and took out a lipstick and a compact, applying a new coat to her lips. Pearl knew Ruby couldn't bear the thought of anyone knowing her relationship with her daughter wasn't perfect.

"That soup ought to be done shortly. I need to grate the cheese and get everything ready while you two talk." Pearl stood up and put Buckley in his bed. As she turned toward the kitchen, he climbed out, ran to the couch, and leaped into Scheri's lap. Ruby gasped.

Pearl turned back to the kitchen, suppressing a laugh. She opened the freezer and extracted a marrow bone from a bag, which she dropped onto his bed to divert his attention from the women on the couch. As expected, he abandoned Scheri's lap.

Chapter 46

Pearl could hear the two of them talking, but focused her attention on lunch preparation. They had a ways to go before they resolved their differences, but this lunch was a good start. Pearl loved Ruby—she was her sister, after all. But the woman lived in an echo chamber filled with people (mostly women) who had the same shallow aspirations as her.

What she valued were things Pearl found superficial. She thought expensive clothes, jewelry, and a huge house in a certain neighborhood were important. Although she'd never worked outside the home, she also hadn't learned to cook very well because they almost always ate in fancy restaurants. A weekly housekeeper kept their home tidy. Pearl didn't know what Ruby did to pass the time other than shopping or eating lunch with her friends. Maybe having her only child rebel had been the wakeup call she needed to tell her there was more to life than frivolous pursuits.

"Why don't you come into town and spend the night? We could have Daddy take us out for dinner at Marché." Ruby ran her perfectly manicured nails through her short, highlighted hairdo.

"I'll think about it," said Scheri. "Right now isn't a good time because I have school and my job, as well as helping Aunt Pearl. Maybe in June."

Ruby's shoulders slumped. The pressure cooker beeped in the background. Scheri jumped up and headed for the kitchen.

"I need to set the table," she said over her shoulder to her mom.

"Oh, I can do that if you two are still talking," said Pearl.

"No, Aunt Pearl. I'll do it."

"You need to wash your hands first, after handling Buckley."

Buckley's ears perked up at the sound of his name, but when no one came his way, he went back to gnawing on his bone.

"Ruby, you can use the bathroom off my bedroom if you want to wash your hands before dinner." Pearl would normally not have said anything, but she knew Ruby's obsession with hygiene, so she acted like she cared, too.

Scheri squeezed a dollop of dish detergent onto her hands, rubbed them together under the kitchen faucet, and dried them on the chicken-patterned dish towel that hung on the refrigerator door. She got out three colorful but mismatched bowls and small plates, soup spoons, and butter knives and carried them to the table. Pearl released the pressure on the pressure cooker and stirred in the shredded cheese and milk. She had already sliced the baguettes. Scheri put the baguettes and the butter dish on the table as Pearl poured the soup into a tureen and added the ladle. She carried it to the table while Scheri brought a pitcher of ice water.

Ruby sat on the couch, rubbing her hands together and observing the two of them from a distance.

"Lunch is ready," said Pearl. "Come in and sit at the table."

They gathered in chairs around the table and served themselves.

"This looks delicious," said Ruby. "Do you have napkins?" Her face drooped and her eyes were puffy, even under the concealer.

Scheri leaped up and tore three paper towels from the roll. She handed one to each of them and sat down again to eat. The room grew quiet except for the sound of chewing.

Pearl ripped a slice of baguette in half and buttered it. "Scheri, did you tell your mother about your job?"

Scheri chewed a bite of bread. "A little."

"She told me she had a job at a small petting zoo company, but that's all." Ruby put down her spoon and turned to Scheri, with eyebrows raised. "Tell me more."

Scheri chewed on the crusty sourdough and took a sip of water before answering. "I work in the office, not with the animals. It's a two-person office. Me and the owner. I, like, answer phones, complete paperwork, file, that kind of thing. It's only part-time, like, three days a week. Mostly it's pretty easy but some days are stressful, especially if I have to talk to an angry customer."

"I'm not surprised you're working in the office. I was astonished when you told me you were working for petting zoo because you never were an animal person."

Scheri jerked her head up and narrowed her eyes at her mother. "What do you mean? You never let me have an animal. How would I even know if I liked them?"

Ruby sputtered. "You-you never acted like you did. They can be so dirty and you've always cared about your appearance. And you had no interest in Pearl's animals when we visited here before. Remember that time when you were about eight and the neighbor's German Shorthair peed on your leg when you were sitting on the front porch? You came in screaming and inconsolable. I think that incident was when you developed an aversion to animals." Ruby twisted the ring on her finger and smiled, recollecting it.

Scheri wasn't smiling. She gripped her butter knife and glared at her mother. "Seriously? Why bring that up? Who *would* want a dog peeing on them? *That's* how you decided I don't like animals?"

"Well..." Ruby stammered.

"No!" Scheri shouted. "*You're* the one who hates animals and you always wanted me to be exactly like you. But I'm not! I love Buckley and the goats. I, like, never had a chance to find out if I cared about animals—because of your obsession with cleanliness. I even had to hide a caterpillar I found under a tree and, like, keep it in a shoebox in the closet till it died, because of you." She leaped up and ran into her room, leaving Pearl and Ruby gaping at each other.

Chapter 47

Ruby's chin trembled and she hunched over her plate, swallowing hard.

"What did I do to turn her against me like this?" She pulled a tissue from her pocket and dabbed at the mascara blackening her cheeks.

Pearl was speechless. She swallowed a spoonful of soup. She hadn't expected things to go so off kilter. She stuffed a piece of bread into her mouth and chewed, thinking of what to say. *Poor Ruby.*

"Honestly, I don't know. It was her idea to invite you out for lunch, so I thought things were improving. Ruby, I have faith you two will get through this." Pearl reached for Ruby's hand. "Separation is painful. And kids don't usually understand how it feels for the parents. I sure didn't when I gave Mom and Dad such a hard time when we were teenagers. But we did get through it. Keep that in mind and give yourself and Scheri time."

Ruby stared at her blankly and shook her hand loose. She dabbed at her tears with the tissue.

"I have to go." She put her napkin on the table and stood up.

"I'm sorry." Pearl rubbed an eyebrow with her index finger. "You don't have to leave yet."

"Yes, I do. I came to spend time with Scheri and apparently she doesn't want to spend time with me," she huffed. Her demeanor had changed and her perfect posture returned. She strode to the couch, lips pressed tightly, and picked up the purse she had left there.

Pearl stood and gave her sister a long hug. "I'll talk to her. Oh, I just remembered. She made us chocolate mousse. She said it's one of your favorites. Let me get you one out of the fridge. You can return the parfait dish any time."

She put a chocolate mousse in a paper bag and handed it to Ruby. "Keep this upright. And drive safely."

Scheri came out of her room with red eyes a few minutes after the driveway alarm went off, signaling that her mother had left the property.

Pearl was putting the rest of the soup in a half-gallon mason jar and the bread in a bag when the bedroom door opened. She saw her niece standing in the doorway. "Help me clean off the table, honey," she said.

Shoulders slumped, Scheri walked to the dining table and stacked the used plates and bowls. She sighed.

"We didn't even get to the chocolate mousse. I wish I hadn't done that, but she triggers me. She talks like she knows me, but it's a fantasy she invented. She's delulu."

"I gave her a chocolate mousse to take home and told her you made it. I thought you'd want her to have one."

Scheri put the ceramic soup bowls and plates next to the sink and put her arms around Pearl. "Thank you, Aunt Pearl. I can always depend on you."

She extricated herself and stood back. "I mean, I guess I'm guilty of fantasy, too—or at least wishful thinking. I thought, like, we'd have a nice lunch and take a walk to the barn so Mom could see the goat babies. I suppose it's just as well we didn't; her reaction would probably have been another disappointment."

"Baby steps. The first step was getting her out for a visit." Pearl rinsed her hands and wiped them with a dish towel while she watched her niece clear off the table.

Pearl didn't think Scheri was being fair to Ruby. She hoped her niece would be more tolerant and her sister would gradually come around. She didn't expect Ruby to touch a goat yet. Just walking out to the barn to see them would be progress. Pearl admitted to herself that even she had had a fantasy of Ruby holding a kid and liking it.

Pearl emptied the partially-eaten soup from the bowls into the compost and added the dishes to the dishwasher. "What time did you say you needed to leave for Junction City?"

"Like, 7:00." Pearl looked at the silver clock on the wall near the door. 3:00.

She handed a damp dishcloth to Scheri. "Here, go clean off the table. We still have time to eat our chocolate mousse, if you want. After that I want you to come out to the barn and help me with chores."

Chapter 48

Pearl watched Scheri from the dusty front window as she got into her car and drove toward the highway. She grabbed Buckley and her purse and sprinted to her Forester. She jumped in and checked the rearview mirror in time to see Scheri's vehicle turn left, toward Junction City.

She dug the keys out of her purse, started the car, backed in by the barn, and headed down the driveway. She would have to keep her distance so she didn't get sighted. Luckily, very little traffic was going east. The cars she met driving west were people coming home from work. She sped up to decrease the distance to Scheri's Lexus, then slowed to avoid getting too close, while keeping her eyes on the car.

Both vehicles decelerated as they drove through Cheshire. A red truck cut in between them from the Dari Mart parking lot, which at first aggravated Pearl. She relaxed a little once she realized her car would be better camouflaged. She sped up again for the last stretch until they reached Highway 99. All three vehicles were stopped at the red light. Pearl's heart pounded and she feared that Scheri would spot her. The big pickup between their cars protected her for now.

"Turn left." She gritted her teeth, talking to the truck in front of her. She didn't want to end up right behind Scheri.

All three vehicles turned left. The Lexus and the pickup sped up to the posted speed of 55 mph. Pearl hung back, wanting to regain some distance. She maintained her speed until she could see Scheri's car by Guaranty RV. By the time she got to the light, it had changed to red after Scheri's car went through the intersection. Pearl had memorized the address of Pasture Pals' office and only had to turn on 3rd Avenue to locate the Lexus.

Pearl went around the block that housed the petting zoo headquarters and parked a block north, figuring they would have to return to Main Street on their way to Lebanon.

Scheri had already parked her car and gone into the business by the time Pearl arrived. She figured the green Dodge Ram in front of Scheri's car belonged to Jeff Broadsky. *It figures. Insecure men drive big trucks.*

Pearl and Buckley waited in the car for ten minutes. She had pulled a sticker out of Buckley's fur when she saw movement by the building out of the corner of her eye. They were on the move. The truck's headlights turned on and the giant vehicle came her direction. Pearl held onto Buckley and ducked across the seats so they couldn't see her when they drove by.

She lifted her head and watched the big vehicle pass by. She needn't worried that she would be seen; Scheri sat in the passenger seat with her head turned toward Jeff. Pearl realized she had been holding her breath. She heaved a sigh of relief and sat up as the truck went left at the next intersection. She started her car and followed.

Once both vehicles were on Highway 99 heading toward Harrisburg, the Dodge Ram sped up to 65 mph. Pearl made an effort to keep up while also staying far enough away that they wouldn't identify her car. She had gotten a ticket on this stretch of road a year earlier so she was hesitant to speed. She caught up again while going through Harrisburg but shortly after that they accelerated and Pearl struggled to keep up.

She reached the outskirts of Lebanon at dusk. Unsure of the area, she hoped she would be able to park near the farm without being spotted. She followed the Ram farther north, on a gravel road, past a mobile home park and five-acre parcels of land that were home to horses, cows, and other livestock. The Pasture Pets farm was one of them.

Pearl watched from a distance as the green truck stopped in front of a property that contained a ramshackle white cottage under a stand of vine maples near the road. She pulled in front of another house catty corner from the farm and turned off her headlights. She didn't see any lights or other sign of life in the old farmhouse, which was set back on the property next to what appeared to be an abandoned apple orchard overgrown with weeds and grass. Pearl figured parking there wouldn't raise any suspicions.

Behind the decrepit house on the petting zoo farm a fenced, wild-looking pasture contained a medium-sized unpainted wooden building with three attached corrals off the side. No animals were visible; they must have been put away for the night.

Pearl sat with Buckley in her lap and kept an eye on the farm as the sun set. Distant lights got closer until a vehicle approached leaving her car awash in bright light. A glance at the rearview mirror showed a white pickup with a canopy blowing up plumes of dust as it approached. She grabbed Buckley and lay across the seat before the truck got too close. It went past them, made a U turn, and parked behind Jeff's truck. With a crescent moon in the sky, Pearl could see an unidentifiable figure emerging from the truck as she peeked over the dash. The driver stayed in the vehicle. The short, overweight passenger had a German Shepherd on a leash.

Pearl shuddered at the sight of the dog. Once the man and dog approached the house, Pearl sat up cautiously. The passenger knocked on the door, stood there for a few minutes, and walked around to the back of the house.

He emerged five minutes later with another man, who resembled Jeff Broadsky. The two of them went to the sidewalk, where the Broadsky guy stopped and the passenger put the dog in the truck cab. When the cab light came on, Pearl got a glimpse of what appeared to be a light-haired person in the driver's seat. The two men went to the back of the truck briefly, and Pearl couldn't tell what they were doing. After a few minutes they returned to the sidewalk. She watched the taller one stride to the house, while the short one lumbered along behind him.

Each man carried a small animal. Buckley's ears perked up at the sound of two high-pitched m-a-a-as and he let out a low growl. They were lambs.

"Stop it, Buckley!" Pearl hissed.

The two figures carried the lambs around the house and vanished behind it.

Pearl yawned. It had been at least a half hour and nothing seemed to be happening. The front door swung open and out came the passenger, walking to the truck. He opened the door, once again lighting up the cab, but not enough for Pearl to definitively identify the driver from that distance. The vehicle's bright lights flashed on, and it veered onto the road from behind Jeff's pickup and came toward Pearl's car. She flattened herself across the seats with Buckley until they had passed her and were a block away.

Pearl realized she needed to get home before Scheri did, but didn't want to leave until she knew her niece was safe. She sat up too late. A woman nearly as tall as Jeff, held the front door open while Jeff and Scheri exited.

Pearl couldn't start the car and drive away now without drawing their attention. She grabbed Buckley and lay across the front seats before headlights lit up her car. The truck passed by, its taillights receding into the darkness as it headed west.

Chapter 49

Pearl raced home as fast as she dared, making it to Junction City in record time. Her mind bounced from one thought to the next. *Why the late-night animal acquisition? Who were the people in the white truck? Would she make it home before Scheri and, if not, what story would she fabricate?*

As she drove through Junction City, Pearl peered down 3rd Avenue to check for Scheri's Lexus in front of the Pasture Pets office. She had lucked out. She saw the car, but also saw Scheri coming out the front door. Pearl's pulse quickened. She would have to be speedy to get home first. She knew Scheri drove too fast because, like many teenagers, she was overconfident.

Hands sweating on the steering wheel, she drove the 30-mph posted speed to the edge of town. She accelerated as the speed limit gradually increased. She turned on Hwy 36 and got up to 60 mph, which she maintained until she got to the reduced speed zone leading up to Cheshire. *This is ridiculous.* On a whim, she pulled into the Cheshire Dari Mart and locked Buckley in the car before going in. She came out a few minutes later with a carton of Tillamook vanilla bean ice cream and put it in the cooler she kept in the back of the car.

She got back on the road and obeyed the speed limit of 55 all the way home. Her heart hammered as she pulled into her driveway and surveyed the parking area. The van was the only car parked there. *Mission accomplished, with time to spare.*

Minutes after she got in the door and put the ice cream away, the driveway alarm buzzed. She carried Buckley out to the porch to see

Scheri driving up in her Lexus. As soon as she got out of her car, Pearl put Buckley down to greet her.

Scheri came up the steps holding Buckley, her cheeks flushed.

"How was the farm?" Pearl did a double take. In the porch light she saw that Scheri wore more makeup than usual—something she hadn't detected earlier.

Scheri couldn't stand still. "I loved all the different animals. Well, except for the llama that spit in my face. I was, like, eating a chocolate-covered coffee bean that Jeff gave me and, apparently, she didn't like it. Gross.

"Did you meet the people who take care of the animals?"

"Oh, yeah. They live on the property. They're a nice couple, probably in their, like, 30s. There was also a guy Jeff was, like, buying lambs from. He had a German Shepherd that didn't seem very friendly. It scared me. I think I prefer small dogs, like Buckley." Scheri rubbed the dog's back, trying to give him the zoomies.

Buckley raced around the living room.

Pearl chuckled. "Crazy critter. Don't get him riled up before bed," she said, trying to appear stern. "Why would someone sell livestock at that time of night?"

Scheri shrugged. "You should see the piglets, Aunt Pearl. Jeff said they're, like, kune kunes. I even got to hold one. We should get some! Of course the goat kids were cute, too. Really, *all* baby animals are adorable."

"Did you look for Daisy?"

Scheri frowned. "Who's Daisy?"

Pearl snorted. "The goat that was stolen from the Skunk Cabbage Festival!"

"Sorry. I'd, like, forgotten about her. I'm not even sure what kind of goat she is. Why would she be there, anyway?" Scheri scraped polish off her fingernail with her thumb.

Pearl shook her head at Scheri's naiveté. "Never mind. Just asking."

Scheri rolled her eyes, finally catching on. "You're so sus. Like, I know Jeff and he wouldn't steal animals. The idea is ridiculous."

Pearl turned to hide her disdain at Scheri's words. They confirmed Pearl's fear that she was enamored with the creep. She steeled herself and turned back to Scheri. She tried to relax her clenched hands.

"Do you know who he gets the animals from?"

"Sort of. He told me on the way to the farm that he was planning to, like, expand the business so we could have more animals and do lots of different events at the same time. Right now we only schedule, like, one or two at the same time. We'll start doing birthday parties and bar mitzvahs, that sort of thing. He said that lots of people, like, can't afford to take care of all the baby animals born so he buys them cheap, because they know the animals will get, like, the best care at the farm."

"Do you know if Pasture Pals microchips or tattoos the animals they buy?"

Scheri's eyebrows creased. "Not that I know of. I haven't seen anything in the accounts about that. Why would they?"

"To prove they own the animals and because it's required for registration. I microchip mine. But I guess if they don't care whether their animals are registered, it probably doesn't matter." Pearl opened her mouth to say something else, but thought better of it. The dreamy look in Scheri's eyes told her the girl was in another world.

Pearl walked into the kitchen and opened the freezer. "Do you want some ice cream before you go to bed? I have some goat milk caramel sauce to put on it."

"Okay," said Scheri, grinning. She twirled and poked at Buckley, trying to stir him up. She acted like a kid at her birthday party, perturbing Pearl.

Pearl got the ice cream out of the freezer and scooped it into two bowls. She put it back and pulled a jar of homemade caramel sauce out of the fridge and scooped a generous amount on top of each bowl of ice cream. Scheri got two spoons out of the drawer and they sat at the table to eat their treat.

Chapter 50

S cheri left for work late Friday morning. She wore a short royal blue skirt and blue-and-white striped tank top after Pearl sent her back into her room to change out of the crop top she'd chosen.

"It's not professional," said Pearl.

"You sound like my mom." Scheri had rolled her eyes and stormed into her room to change.

The odor of perfume wafted through the room, but Pearl decided to say nothing more. *One battle at a time.* She didn't want to drive Scheri closer to Jeff.

The rest of the day was filled with farm chores. Pearl and Westin drove the van to the feed store to replenish hay, grain, and straw for the goats. Inside the feed store, Pearl was reading the label on freeze-dried army fly grubs for her chickens when she heard a grating voice behind her.

"Pearl! We have to stop meeting like this."

Like a fingernail on a chalkboard. She turned to face Zora Vega, and tried to relax her countenance. "Oh, hi. Have you tried these grubs for your chickens?"

"No. My chickens can eat their layer pellets and find their own bugs and worms." Zora laughed. "Hey, are you going to the Rhody Festival this year?"

"No. I never go."

"Oh, you should. It's fun. We go every year for the parade. And, of course, the boys like the rides. And the girls." Zora had closed her eyes, which fluttered open as she finished speaking.

What an irritating habit. I have to get away from her. "Okay, then. Well ... I'm kind of in a hurry, so I have to go pay for my feed. Have fun at the Rhododendron Festival."

Pearl scanned the store for Westin. She walked to the cash register and he joined her there as she ordered and paid for the feed and hay. They got in the van and drove to the outdoor warehouse to pick up their products.

"Did you see Zora?" asked Pearl. "She's so nettlesome."

"Nope. I missed out." He snickered. "What's nettlesome?"

"The word comes from the nettle plant, which causes irritation. A perfect description for her."

THE BARN HAD BEGUN to smell more of manure than fresh straw, attracting flies. After Westin and Pearl unloaded the hay and grain, they got the pitchforks and a wheelbarrow to muck out the buildup. Pearl liked the deep bedding method of adding new hay or straw to the floor all winter because the composting hay kept the goats warmer. She didn't have to spend much for bedding, either. Goats are notorious food wasters, so much of the expensive hay she bought ended up on the floor.

Pearl scooped the top layer of hay and straw into a wheelbarrow while Westin dug out thick layers of the composted grasses. They took turns ferrying the wheelbarrow out to the compost pile on the side of a hill in the pasture.

A half hour in, Pearl shoved the precariously-loaded wheelbarrow out of the barn to the compost pile, nearly spilling its contents due to the weight. She had begun to feel an ache in her knee.

"Let's take a break." She sat on a goat sleeping bench.

"I just want to get it done." Westin leaned against his pitchfork, breathing hard.

"It'll be twice the work if I tip over the wheelbarrow and you have to fill it again. Take a break and hydrate." She walked into the milking room and retrieved the bottles of water she had brought out.

"By the way, Pearl, where'd you guys go last night? I wanted to borrow your hand vac and was surprised when I came out and saw both cars gone."

Pearl looked around the empty barn. "Don't mention it to anyone, but Scheri was going with her boss to the farm in Lebanon where they keep the Pasture Pets animals and Buckley and I followed them."

A smile blossomed on Westin's face. "Do you ever take a day off from sleuthing? And did you find what you were looking for?"

Pearl frowned. "I wasn't really looking for anything. I just don't trust him with Scheri."

Her eyes lit up and she pointed at him. "Will you go with me when I go back to find out if they're keeping Daisy there?"

"I get the feeling I don't have a choice. Let me know when you want to go. And listen, if you want to quit, I can do the rest of the barn by myself."

Pearl pushed the now empty wheelbarrow into position beside him.

"No. They're my goats and I want to do my part." She knew she was the helper on this job and would undoubtedly bow out before they finished.

"Are you doing any work for Jane this weekend?" Pearl retrieved her pitchfork and scooped hay into the wheelbarrow.

"I'm scheduled for tomorrow morning. That is, if my body doesn't give out after this."

Pearl tilted her head and smirked at him.

An hour in, they were about halfway through mucking the does' side of the barn. The goat kids lay sunning themselves in front of the barn, while the older does were out in the pasture.

"My body hurts too much," said Pearl. "I have to go in now. I'll come out and check later so I can help with replacing the lime and straw."

Westin, sporting a thin coat of sweat on his face, glanced up and nodded.

A little more than an hour later, Pearl saw him dragging himself to her house.

"I'm going to the Middle Pass Pub for a few hours after we get the new straw down," he said when she met him at the front door with a glass of ice water.

"You probably need to take a shower first. I can smell your BO from here." She laughed. "Just kidding, but it's probably a good idea."

He and Pearl returned to the barn and finished putting the last bit of straw on the now cleaned floor. The goats came up from the pasture and nibbled the fresh straw on the floor.

"Since you offered, I'll take you up on that shower. The hot water might even help my sore muscles." They put away the pitchforks and wheelbarrow and Westin went to his shed to get clean clothes."

Pearl was refilling the goats' hay and water when Scheri pulled in.

Chapter 51

"I'm going to Valley River Center today so I can get some new clothes," said Scheri.

"It's pretty busy on Saturdays. I can't stand the crowds even on a weekday," said Pearl. "I don't know how you kids can find shopping there entertaining."

Scheri raised her eyebrows. "Grownups." She giggled.

"Did you get paid yesterday?" asked Pearl.

"Yeah. Jeff pays me, like, every two weeks."

"I forgot to ask if you have a bank account, or do you need me to cash your check?"

"He pays me in cash, so I'm good."

Pearl raised an eyebrow. "So he isn't reporting it or taking out taxes and social security?"

"He said it's better for the business that way." Scheri crossed her arms.

Pearl shook her head. *It figures. Better for his business. He probably doesn't report all his income to the government, either.*

"Are you going to buy your own muck boots?" said Pearl.

Scheri laughed. "No. I need new clothes for my job."

No doubt trying to impress Jeff.

"I'll take you to the feed store to get some one of these days. I guess I should pay for them since you're helping me." she said. "Anyway, don't spend all your money in one place." Pearl laughed at her own joke, but Scheri had already turned and was retreating to her bedroom to get ready.

After Scheri left for the mall, Pearl couldn't resist inspecting her room, not sure what she would find. Her niece always kept the door closed. The smell of perfume, body odor, and decaying food hit her when she opened the door. Clothing was strewn all over the floor, with no apparent delineation between clean and dirty. Most of the hangers in the closet were empty. The top of the chest of drawers was cluttered with jewelry, scraps of paper, candy, unwashed dishes, and other items. The corner desk had been converted to a makeup vanity. Mirrors, cosmetics, foundation, perfumes, hair gel, and more covered nearly every square inch. A laptop lay on the bed, which was otherwise a mess of sheets and covers.

Pearl was aghast. It hadn't been this bad the last time she looked in. She had made a mistake assuming Scheri would be neat and clean, and not checking her room more frequently. No wonder she always kept the door shut. Pearl backed out of the room and closed the door behind herself. They needed to have a talk when Scheri got home.

Still clad in her terrycloth bathrobe and cotton pajamas, Pearl took her second cup of coffee out to the porch with Buckley. Brilliant sun radiated from the blue and cloudless sky; it was another glorious day.

Pearl's arms and back ached from mucking the barn the day before. *Westin must be wrecked, since he did the bulk of the work.* She watched the chickens pecking at the scratch she'd thrown on the ground in their run after she had milked the goats.

Her thoughts were interrupted when Buckley let out one bark, jumped from the bench, and ran toward the shed. Westin stepped out, hair awry. He looked toward the house and crouched when he saw Buckley running his way.

"Late for your job at Jane's? You should probably call to let her know if you're still planning to go. In the meantime, would you like a cup of coffee?" hollered Pearl.

He shoved at Buckley, who ran back at him, tail wagging. He picked up the Pomeranian and headed toward Pearl.

"Yes, please. "I got some juicy gossip from the Pub, too. But it'll have to wait till I get my coffee." He grinned and combed his dark hair with one hand.

"You're gonna make me suffer?" she said. "How's your back after all that mucking?"

Westin put the dog on the lawn and flailed his arms. "A little rough."

Pearl went into the house as Westin gingerly ascended the porch steps and sat on the bench. Buckley jumped up next to him.

Pearl came out with the coffee. "Luckily, I'd made a second cup for Scheri, who went to the mall, so all I had to do was microwave it and add the goat milk and sugar."

He took the proffered cup and sipped at it. He looked half-asleep, with glassy, red eyes. His hair stuck out every which-way despite the hand-combing.

How long did you stay at the Pub last night?" said Pearl, sitting down next to him. You look like hell."

Westin put his hand on his forehead. "Too long."

"So what's the gossip? I'm dying to know."

"You know Zora's husband, Tommy? Well, he was at the video lottery machines almost the whole time I was at the Pub. He was like an automaton. I don't get how that's fun, but Dave, the owner, told me he's there almost every night."

Pearl's jaw dropped in surprise. "Wow. Do you think Zora knows? It aggravates me that Dave put those machines in. They're like a tax on the poor and stupid."

"I don't see how she could not know, unless he secretly inherited a fortune." Westin laughed. "And get this. When I told Dave about Kaylee trying to steal one of your goats and how we'd caught her, he said that that Kaylee is Zeus Vega's ex-girlfriend."

Pearl wrinkled her brow and rubbed her chin. "Hmmm. That's interesting."

"That's not all. He also told me he heard Zeus got hauled off to jail yesterday."

Pearl settled back in her seat, feeling vindicated. "What? When? Not that I'm surprised. Like I've been saying, 'I think that kid is up to no good.' Did Dave say what they were charging him with?"

"No one is sure. He said someone told him that Zeus got caught selling drugs to middle school kids."

Pearl's stomach sank. "Drugs?"

"That's what they're saying." Westin shrugged and held out his palms.

"As soon as we're done here, I'm going to go online to check the jail roster to see if he's there. That should list the charges," said Pearl. "I'll let you know what I find out."

"I'll let the chickens out of the run after I shower. They'll appreciate the nice day," said Westin. He finished his coffee and went to get clean clothes from his shed.

When he finished showering, he came out to the porch to find Pearl still sitting there, with paper and pen in hand.

"What're you writing?"

"Just putting down some thoughts I had about the investigation." She closed the notebook and held it up to her chest.

"Sounds mysterious. I guess you don't want to share, so enjoy the rest of the day, and don't get too caught up in trying to find out what happened to Zeus."

"Nope." Pearl shook her head and took another gulp of coffee. She watched him hop down the steps and head for the chicken coop.

She finished her coffee and got up, patting her leg to get Buckley to come with her. He jumped onto the porch and the two of them went into the house. Pearl puttered around the kitchen, putting dirty dishes in the dishwasher and washing off countertops and the table. She wouldn't be surprised if Zeus had been arrested for drugs, but would be disappointed if they didn't also charge him with theft or murder.

She moved to the living room to continue her cleaning. Buckley's shedding had increased in the past month and the rainbow of throw rugs were gradually turning white. Clumps of fur combined with other debris to form dust bunnies in the corners and under the furniture. She pulled the vacuum cleaner out of the utility closet and got to work on that, while the little dog stayed safe on the back of the couch. Every time it came near, he edged away, sure it was coming for him. As Pearl vacuumed, a vision of Zeus being handcuffed and pushed into a police car played in her mind. She felt a strange sense of satisfaction, despite the alleged charges.

With the vacuuming completed, Pearl went into her bedroom and took off her robe, which she hung on a hook on the side of the mahogany antique closet that sat in the corner. She caught an unwelcome glimpse of herself in the mirror that hung on the front of the closet and winced. *I hate being this fat.*

She turned to the four-drawer bureau and dug out a clean pair of gray sweatpants and a well-worn green T-shirt from the 2004 Oregon Country Fair. *Good memories.*

Buckley was perched on the back of the sofa in his favorite viewing spot when Pearl came back into the living room. She sat on the end of the couch and picked up her laptop from the end table. She googled "Lane County Jail," clicked on "inmate search" and typed in Zeus Vega and yesterday's date as the booking date. Nothing came up. She tried the previous day and two days ago. Nothing.

I wonder if he really got arrested?

Unable to sit still, Pearl chewed on her lower lip and tapped her foot, trying to figure out how to get the information she needed. Then she remembered: Zeus is a minor. He would have been lodged at the juvenile detention center, not the jail. *Since that information is confidential, how can I find out if the rumor was true?*

She contemplated calling Zora and asking, but she doubted Zora would tell her anyway. She could call Dan, but she already knew the answer. She would have to wait till the next day when he came over.

She got a large pot out of the cupboard, opened the refrigerator, and removed four half-gallon jars of milk. She needed to use up the milk and cheesemaking helped her relax. And, besides, if she got good enough, she could sell it at the Farmer's Market.

Chapter 52

S cheri came home that afternoon, beaming, with overflowing bags hanging from both arms.

"Did you buy out the stores?" asked Pearl, laughing.

"Very funny, Aunt Pearl." Scheri shook her head and marched through the living room into her bedroom.

"Do I get a fashion show?" yelled Pearl.

Scheri stuck her head out the door. "Sure!"

Three minutes later she paraded into the living room with outfit after outfit. Most were cotton and the colors ranged from sage green to orange to yellow—or, as Scheri informed her: watercress, orangeade, and lemon drop. She modeled shorts, skorts, and leggings with color-coordinated tops, light jackets, and matching sandals. She had purchased a few crop tops, which Pearl planned to prevent her from wearing to work.

When the fashion show ended, Scheri returned to the living room in shredded, light blue denim jeans and a T-shirt advertising a band called Red Dress, which Pearl had never heard of. She flopped onto the couch.

Pearl came out of the laundry room carrying a basket of clean clothes she had gotten from the dryer. "I went in your room while you were gone. How can you live like that? You need to straighten it up after lunch. We have the leftovers from yesterday. I waited, in case you didn't eat yet."

"Yes, we ...I mean ... I had a ham and cheese croissant at the Wooden Cup. Their coffee is surprisingly good for a hick town." Scheri got on her hands and knees and scrambled around the floor with Buckley.

Pearl narrowed her eyes as she set the laundry basket next to the chair in the living room. "Hick town? And what do you mean *we*?"

Scheri's face turned crimson. "Oh, I ran into Jeff in town so we decided to eat together." She avoided Pearl's gaze.

Pearl shook her head. She sat in the overstuffed chair and folded the clean laundry that she placed on the empty coffee table. *Ruby would be horrified if she had even an inkling of Scheri having a crush on a man 10 years older.* At least she hoped it was only a crush.

Alarm showing on her face, Scheri stumbled to correct her lie. "He's my boss. I don't see what the big deal is."

"I didn't say anything about a big deal. You're the one who decided to keep your meeting a secret." Pearl looked down and silently folded laundry.

Scheri thrust out her chin. "Can we drop it?" she pleaded.

Pearl nodded and sighed. *Parenting a teenage girl isn't easy.* She felt a little more sympathy for Ruby.

"I suppose. Now will you help me with this laundry? Part of it's yours. I did it the last time, but you need to take on some of the work in the house. And put it in the dresser drawers when you're done, instead of adding to the mess in there."

Scheri brought a chair from the dining table and sat next to Pearl. She dug through the plastic laundry basket and pulled out a couple of her shirts. They folded clothes until they had emptied the basket. Scheri carted her pile of clothing to her room and Pearl put hers back in the basket, which she lugged into her bedroom.

She came out with the empty basket and returned it to the laundry room.

"Aunt Pearl," said Scheri when Pearl came back into the living room, "I was thinking we should, like, go to the Rhododendron Festival in Florence tomorrow since the weather is gonna be nice.

Pasture Pals will be there with some of the animals. I saw it on the schedule. You can meet Jeff, too."

"Did you tell him we're coming?"

"No, I didn't know if you'd want to go and thought we could surprise him if you did." Scheri twirled a strand of hair around her index finger and looked at Pearl questioningly.

Pearl realized she had been holding her breath and let it out in a rush. *He will definitely be surprised.*

"That sounds fun. I'll bet you just want to wear some of your new clothes, don't you?" Pearl teased.

Scheri crossed her arms and frowned. "No, that's not it. I thought we could get off the farm for a day and do something different."

"I was kidding." She nudged Scheri playfully. "I think it's a great idea. I've never been to the Rhody Festival. I always considered it a biker get-together, based on the number of motorcycles roaring by on the highway every year at this time. But I'm game."

Pearl had an idea. *It was time to make a phone call once Scheri went to bed.*

Chapter 53

The drive to Florence Sunday morning was glorious. They had the road mostly to themselves. The Siuslaw River meandered along to their right, parallel with the highway. Meadows bloomed with purple camas, blueberry bushes were coming to life, and farms featured horses, goats, cows, or chickens. Acres of fir trees lined the road, some lying on the ground, leaning against each other, or cut into smaller pieces—the detritus of the ice storm they had had earlier in the year.

Acres of clearcut forests scarred the landscape in various places along the road. Pearl didn't think she would ever accept the fact that she had made her home in the middle of a giant tree farm owned mostly by logging companies.

Fluffy marshmallow clouds filled the sky, a respite from the grayness that brought what had seemed to be endless spring rains. Pearl took her time, driving 45 mph on the winding road. Scheri peered out the window, pointing out huge rocks in the river and reading out the names of towns—Deadwood, Tide, Brickerville—as they headed toward the Pacific Ocean.

"Let's go check out the rhododendron display before we do anything else. That's the main purpose of the festival after all, isn't it?" said Pearl. "I'm glad these modern cell phones have such good cameras on them. I want to get some pictures. I don't dare plant any rhododendrons or azaleas on the farm because they're so poisonous to goats, but I do think they're pretty. I can enjoy them as pictures on the walls of my house." She chuckled.

"We need to make sure we finish with the flowers before noon so we can get to Old Town and find parking before the parade," said Scheri. "I looked it up online."

Scheri wore ripped-up black jeans, along with the new orangeade-colored crop top and flip flops she had purchased at the mall the day before. Pearl had mentioned that she'd be cold in that outfit, but when you're sixteen, looking cute trumps being warm. She had spiked up her dyed black hair with gel and applied eye makeup a little darker than normal.

Pearl, who lived in sweatpants and T-shirts or sweatshirts, had managed to find some flowered leggings and a sage blouse. She had pinned her hair up in a messy bun held by a gold metal clip. She had located a passable pair of sneakers that wouldn't give her a blister walking in them for hours.

The Three Rivers Casino sign told them they were almost to Florence. They followed the winding road until they made a left turn to get to the Florence Events Center.

After parking the Forester in the half-filled lot, they went into the Center where they were greeted by tables full of rhododendrons in a rainbow of colors.

They wandered through the displays for a half hour. Scheri lagged behind, having lost her interest in flowers before Pearl did.

"We need to get to Old Town before the parade starts," Scheri said.

Pearl pulled out her cell phone and checked the time. "You're right. I think I've seen enough anyway."

They walked back through the displays and out the front door. In no time at all, they were in Old Town.

Chapter 54

They reached Old Town Florence at 11:45. Pearl could see why Jane had suggested that they leave early. They drove from one full parking lot to another, keeping an eye on street spaces. No luck. They drove several blocks, parked on the street, and hurried to the parade route. Pearl assigned her niece to remember where they had parked—something she was notoriously terrible at.

The two women walked toward town and past the area where the parade had formed. There were so many people! Pearl gazed at the carnival rides on the Siuslaw River waterfront; they obviously had a bigger budget than Middle Pass. Her stomach roiled as she considered the Zipper and she felt dizzy upon seeing the Ferris wheel. She hoped Scheri didn't expect her to go on any rides. *Why pay to get sick?*

A marching band, brightly-decorated jalopies, and go-carts started to roll down the crowd-lined streets only a few minutes after they got there. The first-arrivals sat on lawn chairs and blankets on the edges of the road. Children jumped in delight with each entry. Huge floats decorated with vibrant rhododendrons crawled by, followed by a school marching band, a phalanx of motorcycles, Eugene Pro Rodeo horses and riders, and Shriners. Excitement rippled through the air.

As the last entry in the parade approached the end of the route, sightseers folded lawn chairs, picked up blankets, and huge crowds pushed through in the opposite direction. Pearl grabbed Scheri's arm so they wouldn't become separated and they made their way toward the restaurants on Main Street.

"I'm starving," said Scheri. "Let's get something to eat. After my stomach is full we can find the petting zoo and Jeff."

"We have to go to Mo's Seafood and Chowder," said Pearl. "It's part of a trip to Florence." They headed away from the water to Mo's where they were added to a waiting list.

"We'll be here all afternoon," Scheri complained, clutching her stomach. "I'm starving."

"You'll survive," said Pearl, laughing. "I'm sure they hired extra staff for the festival and the line will move fast."

Scheri pouted.

Ten minutes later Pearl heard her name called. A server escorted them to a small table in the packed restaurant.

"See, that wasn't so bad." Pearl took the menus proffered by a waitress and sat on the seat facing the window.

"Do you know what you want to drink or should I wait until I take your order?"

Pearl read her name tag. "I already know what I want, Angie. The Shrimp Louie. How about you, Scheri?"

"I need more time," said Scheri. "But I'll have a strawberry lemonade."

"Just water for me," said Pearl.

The smiling waitress returned a few minutes later with their silverware and drinks and took their orders.

Scheri excused herself to go to the bathroom. As soon as Pearl saw the door close behind her, she pulled out her cell phone.

"Hi. I'm calling to make sure you made it," she said when the person answered.

"Okay. I'll let you know when we need to meet. We're at Mo's right now and should be done within 45 minutes or so. Will you be free?"

"Okay. I have to go before Scheri gets back. See you then." She hung up the phone and put it back in her purse.

Chapter 55

"There it is!" said Scheri, pointing to the vendor booth near the far edge of the festival grounds. A heavyset woman sat in a small wooden box office at the front of a fenced-off 15x30-foot area. She sold little cups of peanuts to feed the animals. A line of people stretched along the fence on the side.

Pearl scanned the area, but saw no sign of Jeff.

"C'mon." Scheri took her arm and pulled her forward. Pearl watched her eyes light up as they rushed toward the petting zoo.

"Do you know the woman selling peanuts?"

"No. I haven't met anyone who works the events."

"Let's go in and see the animals before we try to find Jeff, okay? said Pearl.

Scheri surveyed the area. Her shoulders slumped when she didn't see him. "Okay. Maybe he went to get something to eat."

They were fifth in line behind a mother with three dirty little boys who looked under the age of seven or eight. The kids whined and fidgeted, as people already in the pen took their time petting and feeding the animals. The line grew.

"If you don't stop it, we're gonna go home and forget about seeing the animals at all," hissed the mother.

"No! Please. We want to pet the animals." said the older two boys in unison.

The youngest bawled. "I'm thirsty."

"If you don't stop crying, I'll give you something to cry about." The mother grabbed his arm. "You won't die of thirst before we're done at the petting zoo."

He sobbed harder, mucus, tears, and dirt mixing on his face. The other two kids stood next to him with bored expressions.

Pearl balled her fists and glared at the mother, who didn't notice her.

Scheri tensed up and froze, gaping at the family. "I never want kids," she said. She broke her gaze and again searched the area for Jeff.

"Hey, there's the llama that spit on me the night I went over to the farm." She wrinkled her nose, pointing at the tall furry animal in the pen.

Pearl chuckled. She didn't trust llamas, or other large animals, for that matter.

Parents and children exited the petting zoo and the line crawled along as new groups purchased peanuts and entered. Pearl tried to scrutinize the animals, but the pen was too crowded for her to see any of them very well with so many people moving through.

Finally they made it to the front of the line. They bypassed the 50 cent peanuts. Pearl worried about the animals overeating and getting sick. She wasn't about to add to the problem.

As they entered the door that swung into the enclosure, Pearl observed Scheri fussing with her hair.

"Do I look okay?" asked Scheri.

Pearl scoffed. "I'm sure the animals won't notice," she muttered.

They pushed their way between people, carefully watching the ground as they stepped along the wood chips in an attempt to avoid the inevitable poop. They stopped to watch the ducks and chickens in an area to their right. Scheri seemed distracted, looking toward the trailer behind the pen repeatedly.

Pearl made herself as small as she could, hoping to avoid contact with the other visitors. *There shouldn't be so many people in here at one time.*

They moved toward the back of the petting area where goat kids and lambs were milling around between people. One of the kids caught

Pearl's eye. A little black-and-white one, that tried to get out of the way of the crowd. *What were the odds?*

Pearl caught up to the goat and reached around it to hold it in place. She squatted next to the frightened kid and looked under it to determine if it was a male or female. *A female.* She examined the goat's sides, noting a large black spot on each of them. *Black tail, black mustache.* She pulled out the microchip reader she had brought along and scanned the goat's tail web, checking the readout against a scrap of paper she had written a number on. *It was definitely Daisy!*

"What are you doing?" Scheri looked confused.

Pearl stuffed the microchip scanner and paper into her purse. She feared that if she said something and Scheri repeated it to Jeff, he would find a way to hide the doeling before the sheriff could get there. *I've been one step behind these thieves since the goat show and I'm not about to let her go now.*

Before Pearl could answer, Scheri looked toward the back of the pen, her attention caught by something else.

"Jeff!" she yelled. She pushed her way through the crowd toward the petting zoo's rear exit, oblivious to Pearl and the goat.

Pearl saw Jeff Broadsky walking in front of the small green-and-white travel trailer behind the petting zoo enclosure. He jerked his head around at the sound of Scheri's voice. His eyes widened and, with a huge smile on his face, he waved her over. He didn't notice Pearl, and Scheri seemed to have forgotten she existed.

While Scheri moved through the crowd to get to the back gate, Pearl crouched behind the llama, which was only a few feet away, pulled out her cell phone and dialed.

"Dan, come to the petting zoo right now!" she whispered. "Jeff Broadsky is here. I knew it. I found Daisy, too."

Chapter 56

Pearl stood and made her way to the exit, sidestepping animals and children. She could see Jeff with his arm around Scheri's shoulder. He was talking animatedly just a few inches from her face, with a big smile on his face. She leaned into him. Pearl bristled. *Just as I feared.*

She continued her path toward the two of them.

Jeff glanced at her and did a double take. "Not you again!" His grin turned into a frown.

Scheri turned and, seeing her aunt, she gasped in alarm and astonishment and slid out from under his arm. She looked from Pearl to Jeff, confused. Her face reddened as Pearl walked to her side.

"You know my Aunt Pearl?"

"This is the aunt you've been talking about?" he said, scowling. "We met at the Skunk Cabbage Festival."

A short, chubby dark-haired teenage boy emerged from behind the petting zoo fencing, oblivious to the drama going on.

"Hi, Z!" said Scheri, smiling.

It was Zander. *Zora can't be far away. Today really is my lucky day.*

Zander nodded at Scheri, not noticing Pearl, and faced Jeff. "We need to talk to you about money for a minute," he said.

Jeff's face went white. Pearl glimpsed Zora standing behind Zander at the side of the trailer. Zora couldn't see Pearl.

"I'll be back in a minute," Jeff said to Scheri. He grabbed Zander's arm and shoved him and Zora behind the trailer.

With Scheri's attention on Jeff, Pearl slid her phone out of her purse and turned on the voice recorder app. She held it behind her back and touched Scheri's arm with her other hand. "That little girl must really like the llama. But I don't think that's allowed."

Scheri turned to watch a mother lifting her child onto the llama's back. Her eyes flicked to the edge of the trailer but the trio had disappeared from view.

"Go tell her not to do that," said Pearl. "You're in charge now since Jeff's busy."

Scheri walked to the fence to stop the mother. Pearl backed to the edge of the trailer and held her phone behind her back to pick up the sound of the voices.

"We came to get the rest of the money for the animals we sold you," said Zora.

"This isn't a good time," Jeff hissed. "You can come to the office tomorrow."

"I don't know if you heard, but Zeus is in jail, so he couldn't come. We need money for his bail," pleaded Zora.

Pearl was elated. She hoped her recorder was picking up the voices.

"I didn't want Zeus here, either. It's not my problem he got arrested. There is something you can do for *me,* though. That old woman out there has been nosing around looking for the black-and-white Nigerian you sold me—and I made the mistake of bringing it today. I had no idea she'd be here."

"What old woman?" Zora lowered her voice. "What're you talking about?"

"Scheri's aunt!" He spit out.

"What? Where is she?" Zora sounded alarmed. As she moved toward the corner of the trailer, Jeff jerked her back.

"Don't let her see you! Zander, go out there right now and get that black-and-white goat out of the enclosure and take her out of the festival. I'll distract the woman," Jeff whispered. "And do it now!"

Pearl saw Zander come out from the other side of the trailer. She watched him let himself into the exit gate, forgetting the phone in her hand. Zora and Jeff appeared from the left side of the trailer behind her as Scheri returned from confronting the woman.

"Oh, Pearl, you came," said Zora, walking up from behind her. Pearl turned at the sound of her voice and stuffed the phone into her purse. She momentarily took her eyes off Zander.

"Hey, what's going on?" came a woman's voice from the petting zoo enclosure. "Put that goat down!"

They all turned toward the enclosure and saw Zander carrying Daisy toward the exit. A short-haired, stocky woman in shorts and a tank top held on to the back of his T-shirt, stretching it. He jerked to loosen her grip, stumbling over a woman crouched with a toddler to pet a piglet. He regained his balance and, with a lunge, pushed open the exit gate and whirled toward the parking lot. His eyes were wild.

The sheriff, a deputy, and two Florence police officers appeared through the crowd. Pearl, Scheri, Zora, and Jeff watched the action, open-mouthed.

"Stop. Goat thief!" yelled the stocky woman. The two police officers moved to the side of the petting zoo to intercept him. In a panic, Zander shoved his way through the crowd and crashed into the box office, nearly knocking it over. Cups of peanuts flew off the counter onto the dusty ground. People standing in line leaped backward to avoid a collision with him.

Zander lurched to the right, slipping past them, and ran into the crowd. The two officers chased him, gaining ground as he staggered from the weight of the goat. All of them soon disappeared from view.

Screams and shouts emanated from the crowd: "Hey, watch where you're going!" "Ow, get off of me." "What's going on?" The sounds became more distant.

Jeff froze. He licked his lips and glared.

The sheriff and his deputy walked along the petting zoo fence until they were facing Jeff and Zora. Zora's hands were shaking and she looked back and forth from the crowd to the sheriff and deputy.

Jeff put on his electric smile and cocked his head to the side. "He was stealing a goat. It's a good thing you guys were there to stop him. I really appreciate it."

"Don't play coy with the officers! You put him up to it." Pearl looked at him with venom. She remembered her phone was still recording. She pulled it out of her purse and pressed the stop button.

"I have the evidence right here, Sheriff," she said, holding her phone in the air. "Zora came to get paid for the stolen animals they sold him. Jeff admitted that he had purchased Daisy and told Zander to sneak her out while he distracted us."

"Calm down. We can handle this," said Dan. He winked at Pearl.

"You're both under investigation for livestock theft. You need to come with us now," the Sheriff said to Jeff and Zora. Zora looked around frantically but had nowhere to go.

Jeff rubbed the back of his neck. "Livestock theft?"

"No!" Scheri stared at the sheriff in disbelief. "You must have the wrong person."

"Oh, he's the right person, Scheri," said Pearl. "Those lambs you saw being delivered to the farm in Lebanon when you were there? Those were most likely stolen. And so was Daisy! How do you think Daisy got here?"

Scheri opened her mouth in shock. She gazed at Jeff, tears welling in her eyes. "This isn't true, is it?"

"I'll explain later, babe," he said to Scheri, as the police officer handcuffed him. "Don't worry. It's a mistake."

"We only sold our own animals," said Zora.

Pearl bristled. "I know you killed Annie, too, Zora. I've never been overly fond of your but I didn't think you were that evil."

Dan looked at Pearl, shook his head and mimed zipping his lips. She looked down, knowing she had done it again.

Zora's nostrils flared. "I didn't mean to. All I wanted to do was get Daisy back. It was an accident." She looked defiant.

"Zora, before you say any more, I need to read you your Miranda rights." The Sheriff recited her rights while Zora glared at him.

"I want a lawyer."

The two law enforcement officers returned with Daisy and a handcuffed, chastened Zander. The knees of his jeans were dirty and ripped and one palm was skinned and bleeding. A crowd of festival-goers grew, their interest piqued.

"Please go back to enjoying the festival, folks," said Dan in a loud voice. "We have everything under control."

He turned to the officer carrying Daisy. "For now you can put her back in with the other animals. We'll sort things out later."

"Let's get another car here and take them all to the police department," he commanded the officers. "We'll sort out the jurisdictional issues after I get there. And Ms. Vega has invoked her rights, so hold off on questioning her."

"Zander, too," said Zora defiantly. "He's a minor."

Chapter 57

"Let's go get a cold drink and sit for a few minutes," said Pearl. She led Scheri toward a concession stand and ordered two medium lemonades. They walked to an empty green metal bench near the music stage and sat down. Scheri appeared shell-shocked, her gaze wandering absently.

"Before we go, I have to call Lindy to let her know we found Daisy. I don't want to wait until we get home." Pearl pulled out her cell phone and chose Lindy's number from her contact list.

"Lindy? I'm in Florence at the Rhody Festival right now and you'll never guess who's here," said Pearl. "No. Are you sitting down? Daisy. My niece talked me into coming today and I found her in Pasture Pets Petting Zoo.

"Yes, I know it's her. All the markings match and I even brought my microchip reader. It matches her number. She didn't seem too happy, but once she gets back to Sierra, I'm sure she'll be a joyous little kid in no time."

She could hear Lindy cover the receiver and talk to someone. A happy shriek told Pearl it was Sierra.

"I still need to find out the procedure for dealing with the animals here. The Florence police and the Sheriff know the situation. She may have to go into temporary custody, but I'll do everything I can to get her home to you as soon as possible. Will you do me favor and fax the flyer with her picture and information to the Florence Police Department?"

As they waited for a decision by the police about whether they could take Daisy home, Scheri sat, with red-rimmed eyes, staring vacantly at the throngs of festival-goers passing by.

"Wh-what's gonna happen to Jeff?" she finally murmured to Pearl.

"I don't know. They'll have to determine whether any of the other animals he has were stolen. It will depend on his involvement and whether he has a prior record." Pearl made a mental note to check online for any prior arrests he had. "But you can plan on being out of a job."

Scheri shook her head in disbelief and her eyes welled with tears again. She brushed at the dirt around a rip in her jeans.

"He seemed so nice," she said in a weak voice. "And what about Z and Mrs. Vega? Do you really think she murdered someone?"

Pearl nodded and patted her niece's leg. "I do. I know you're disappointed about Jeff, sweetie."

Pearl's cell phone rang. It was good news. After some finagling—and intervention from Dan—she had gotten the police department to let her take Daisy home.

"I have to get a tarp to put in the car so we can transport Daisy. Do you want to go with me or wait here?"

"I guess wait here," said Scheri in a flat voice. She sat hunched on the bench, arms wrapped around herself, holding back tears.

Pearl rushed to her car and drove to the Ace Hardware store she had seen when they came into town. She purchased a blue tarp and headed back to Old Town, where she found a temporary parking spot near the petting zoo. She got out of the car and opened the rear door. She unwrapped the tarp and spread it out in the back of the vehicle and draped it over the back seats.

She summoned her dejected niece to the car. "Stay here while I go get the goat. If anyone questions you about being parked here, let them know why we're in this space and that it's temporary."

Pearl walked over to the fenced area and talked to a police officer. Within minutes, she returned to her car with the officer, who carried Daisy. Pearl directed him to the back of the car and he placed the complaining kid on the tarp.

The officer told her a group of volunteers with trucks would arrive later to take the remaining animals to the homes of people who temporarily housed seized farm animals.

After she thanked the officer, Pearl drove out of the parking spot and circled back to Highway 101 for the drive home. Daisy stood in the back of the Subaru for the whole trip and cried from time to time.

All Pearl could think of was how Sierra and Lindy would react when she got there with Daisy.

Pearl and Scheri were a study in contrasts during the drive back to Middle Pass. Scheri sat mute, staring at her hands. Her face was splotchy and her cheeks were streaked with black mascara from the tears she couldn't hold back. Even the presence of a cute goat kid in the back didn't improve her mood.

While Pearl empathized with Scheri's misery, the joy she felt at finding Daisy overwhelmed it. Despite her elation, she tried to tamp down her enthusiasm in front of her niece.

Pearl licked her lips, thrilled that Jeff Broadsky had been implicated in the scheme. She had not trusted the guy since the first day she met him and she knew Ruby would never have forgiven her if Scheri had gotten trapped any further in his web. She realized it had already gotten out of hand when she witnessed them wrapped around each other earlier.

By the time they got to Mapleton, the silence was deafening.

"Do you want to talk?" Pearl glanced over at her. Neither of them was enjoying the scenery like they had on the way to the festival.

Scheri shook her head. "Can we turn on the radio?"

Pearl punched the on button. "Sure. Pick whatever station you'd like."

Scheri pushed the numbered buttons until she found the popular music station. Not exactly what Pearl would select, but if it made Scheri feel better....

The rest of the drive went quickly, with the road mostly empty. Groups of motorcycles passed them intermittently, probably on their way home from the Rhody Festival. Pearl knew Highway 126 would have been a nightmare of heavy car and motorcycle traffic as people returned inland from the coast after the weekend.

Chapter 58

Pearl heard Buckley yipping as soon as she opened the car door. They had been gone for less than seven hours but you'd think it had been a week, as frantic as he sounded. After Pearl put in the driveway alarm, Buckley had figured out that when it went off someone would soon appear at the house. *Westin better have let him out at least once that day.*

Scheri got out of the car without a word, shuffled to the house, and opened the front door. Buckley came flying out and, even in her despondent mood, she perked up and grabbed him. She held him to her chest until he licked her face. She laughed and put him back on the ground. He ran to Pearl, who had opened the back of the car to get Daisy out.

The door to Westin's shed opened and out he came. His eyes widened as he saw Pearl at the back of the vehicle trying to coax a goat out. He strode over to the car.

"Need some help?" he said. "You didn't buy another goat, did you?"

He looked at the black-and-white doeling and his eyes widened. "Wait. That's not Daisy, is it?"

Pearl beamed. "Yes, it is. Will you help me get her out of the car? I'll tell you all about it later. And I hope you let Buckley out to get some exercise today."

Westin folded his arms across his chest. "Of course I did!"

Daisy backed as far as she could into the corner of the hatch, eyeing Buckley. Pearl bent down, ruffled Buckley's fur, and picked him up for a minute.

"Go in the house," she commanded as she placed him on the grass. Surprisingly obedient, he ran to the house and Scheri.

Pearl put the dog leash she kept in the car around Daisy's neck. Westin leaned over and put one arm around her chest and the other around her belly and lifted the kid out of the car to the ground. Pearl walked her to the barn, with Westin behind her to push when she stopped. He got in front of Pearl to open and close the barn door and the gate, so Daisy could be led to an empty stall. The Hidden Creek Farm goats came over to stare at the interloper. Pearl went back out the gate and came back with a bucket of fresh water and some timothy hay for her.

Pearl had to separate Daisy not only because her goats might beat up the stranger, but because she didn't know what the kid had been exposed to during her time at the farm and petting zoo. The Langs would most likely quarantine her for a month at their farm to make sure she was healthy after being exposed to other animals.

Pearl's goats, who had spent most of the day browsing in the pasture, looked at her as if to ask "Where's our food?" She chuckled and filled their hay feeders and refreshed their water buckets. She would return to milk the goats after she had eaten and made phone calls to get everyone up to speed regarding what had happened. She also wanted to call and thank Dan for showing up at the Rhody Festival. This time he had believed her. Or at least he had gone along with the plan. The main thing was that he had her back when she needed him.

Chapter 59

When Pearl got back in the house after doing chores, Scheri was still in her room. Pearl knocked on her bedroom door and asked if she was okay. She heard Scheri mumble that she was cleaning her room, "like you wanted." Pearl gave her space, thinking she needed to get over her heartbreak and come to terms with the fact that Jeff was not a good guy.

Later that afternoon, Scheri's bedroom door swung open and she came out, silent as a ghost. She sat on the couch, wordless, but restless as a bird in a cage. Something was different. Pearl did a double take and realized she hadn't seen the girl without makeup before. *She must be pretty distraught to not be wearing makeup.*

Scheri swallowed hard. "How did you, like, figure out that Jeff had Daisy?"

Pearl sat across from her and tried to modulate her voice. "It's a long story, but here goes. Even though I didn't know for sure that he had her, I'd suspected Jeff was involved for quite a while. When I first met him at the Skunk Cabbage Festival, I got a bad feeling right off the bat. He showed no sympathy for Daisy being stolen and he didn't really strike me as an animal lover."

Scheri sat, sullen, her lips pressed into a fine line. She jiggled one leg.

"I had some misgivings about you going to work for him, but I thought you needed the employment experience and he was probably harmless, so I agreed. By the way, I searched him online and he lied about starting the company; either his dad or uncle actually started it when Jeff was just a kid." She raised her eyebrows.

"Why didn't you tell me?"

Pearl sighed. "Two reasons: I thought you wouldn't believe me and, does it really matter? I found out he's a braggart, but I didn't think it would necessarily affect your job."

Scheri gazed at her hand, picking at a nail.

Pearl settled into the chair. "When you said you were going to the farm with him that night, I got nervous about whether he was really taking you there. The more time went by, the less I trusted the guy. So I decided to follow you to make sure you were safe. I also figured I'd find out where the farm was located and maybe go back later and see if Daisy was being kept there."

Scheri flinched. "What? Like, you followed us there?"

"Yes."

"How did you do that without us, like, seeing you?"

"Probably because you were looking at each other and not the traffic."

Scheri rolled her eyes.

"After you got to the farm, I parked a few houses away and we just watched and waited."

"Who's we? Your precious Dan?" Scheri curled her lip.

"No," Pearl laughed, "my precious Buckley. After a little while a pickup truck pulled up. I couldn't tell who was driving, other than a short person with light hair. That was one of my first clues. Zander had made a comment that Zeus refused to ride with anyone else, and it wasn't his truck so I knew it was someone else. I watched the passenger go to the house, come back with Jeff, and take two lambs in. I could tell by the walk and squat body that it was Zander. He also had a German Shepherd, which I figured was the one that had scared me at the Vega farm." Out of the corner of her eye, she could see Scheri's lips pursed as she listened.

"That dog is aggressive," Scheri mumbled. "I can see why it would scare you."

Pearl nodded and smoothed her pant legs.

"How did you know Z—I mean, Zander's mom was involved?"

"I went to Zora's farm because I suspected Zeus of stealing Daisy and thought she might be there. She wasn't, but when I was there, I noticed a stack of overdue bills on a table in the living room. Then Westin told me he saw Tommy Vega at the Pub the other night, losing money on the video lottery machines and Dave, the owner, said he has a gambling problem. That explained the unpaid bills, but I still hadn't figured it out.

"After we caught Kaylee, the girl who tried to steal Beyoncé, I thought maybe it was her. Then Westin told me he found out she was Zeus's ex. I started to wonder if she was the girl in the park with Zeus the day Daisy was stolen. Everything kept pointing to the Vega family, but I still thought it was Zeus.

"When you told me what Jeff said about people who needed money being willing to sell their livestock for low prices, a light bulb went off in my head. At that point, I wondered if Zora might have put Zeus up to it. That still left the question of who murdered Annie and why.

"When I talked to the farmer next door to the Spink farm after I found her body, I learned that Annie had recently been given a black-and-white miniature goat kid—he called it a Dwarf Pygmy. My theory was that Zeus gave Daisy to Annie to hide her when he learned we weren't going to abandon our investigation until we found her. But how would he know that unless Zora told him? I also told her I was going to Annie's to look for Daisy, so I think they panicked and went to take her back before I could get there.

"The farmer next door told me he saw a gray car leaving after he heard arguing coming from Annie's farm. Zora drives a silver Ford Focus, so I figured he probably confused silver and gray. Zeus only drives his truck and Zander doesn't drive.

"Despite my misgivings, all the evidence was pointing to Zora as the murderer. Of course, the DNA results were the only way to know for sure, until Zora blurted out a confession.

"When I saw Zander with lambs at the Pasture Pets farm in a truck with a driver that could possibly be Zora, I figured he was involved, too. They don't raise sheep, so the lambs couldn't have been his. I was surprised because I thought he was a good kid. I should have known better since nothing Zora says is true.

"So after you invited me to go to the Rhody Festival I asked Dan to meet me there. I didn't expect to find Daisy, but I knew Jeff was involved in buying stolen animals.

"I had no idea everything would come together like it did. Zora had told me she was going to the Rhody Festival parade, but with all the people there I had no idea if I'd see her. Dan and I knew there was a good chance we wouldn't find anything and, if that was the case, we'd meet up for coffee or something."

Scheri wrinkled her nose.

Pearl put her hands on her hips. "Oh, come on, Scheri. There's nothing wrong with Dan."

"No comment." Scheri looked up and shook her head.

Pearl snorted and continued, "I have to admit I was pleasantly surprised to find Daisy in the petting zoo. Zora made a huge mistake selling her to Jeff. Either she panicked and needed to get rid of the evidence after killing Annie or she didn't consider that someone might recognize Daisy at a public event. I don't think she even knew Jeff had brought her that day. And neither of them had any idea I would be there looking. In fact, I told Zora I wasn't going to the Rhody Festival."

Scheri rubbed her temples. "How do you know that Jeff was, like, aware that the animals he was buying were stolen?"

"First of all, you'd have to be living in a cave to not know about all the thefts in the area; they were reported in the paper and on the local news. Is he that stupid? If I were running a petting zoo, I'd make darn sure the animals were legit.

"Second, I got him on tape when Zander and Zora were demanding that he pay them. And he *knew* he had Daisy or he wouldn't have told Zander to get her out of there. That was his final mistake."

Scheri wrapped her arms around herself and her eyes welled up with tears. "I feel like a fool for believing him. Do you think he really even liked me?"

"I'm sure he did, honey. But he isn't the kind of guy you want to get involved with. You need someone trustworthy. Don't worry. You have plenty of time to find a boyfriend. Your mom is right about that.

"Now, after you eat, why don't you go out with the goats and soak up some of their calming energy?"

Chapter 60

Pearl waited until 10 am the next morning to start breakfast. She hoped to cheer Scheri up with raspberry and whipped cream crepes. Ten thirty rolled around without a peep from Scheri. Pearl went to the bedroom door and knocked quietly. No answer. She knocked a little harder and called, "Scheri, are you awake?"

Hearing nothing, Pearl turned the doorknob and opened the door a crack. The room was cleaner than she had seen it, except for the sheets that had been stripped from the bed and were lying on the floor in a pile. Noticeably missing were Scheri's suitcase, backpack, and morass of cosmetics. Pearl went in and opened the closet door. Her clothes were gone, too. The dresser drawers were empty. A note was on the nightstand next to the bed. She picked it up and read:

Dear Aunt Pearl,

I'm sorry I had to leave like this. I really appreciate you letting me stay here and teaching me about the goats. I feel so stupid falling for Jeff and all his lies. I realized last night that I need to be back with my family. There's also no point in my staying here now since I don't have a job. I have a better chance of getting one in Eugene anyway. I promise to keep in touch and to come out and visit you and Buckley, and Beyonce, Taylor, and the other goats.

Say goodbye to Westin for me and give Buckley a hug.

Love, Scheri

Pearl must have been sleeping soundly to have missed the driveway alarm when Scheri left. She felt a little sad about her going, but also relieved. She had begun to feel in over her head managing a teenager.

She'd call her sister later to make sure that Scheri had made it home. In the meantime, it looked like she would be eating raspberry crepes alone.

Chapter 61

T hat afternoon, after Sierra and Daisy were reunited, Sheriff Dan arrived at Hidden Creek Farm, clean half-gallon canning jar in hand. Pearl opened the front door a crack and let Buckley, the official greeter, race out to meet him.

She welcomed the two of them in, put the jar on the counter, and offered tea to Dan and a dog biscuit to Buckley. After everyone was situated—Dan and Pearl on the couch in the living room and Buckley in his dog bed—they recounted the prior day's events.

Dan's eyes twinkled. "That was quite an adventure yesterday," he said. "How's Scheri doing today?"

"When I got up this morning she had left," said Pearl. Dan raised his eyebrows in surprise.

"She left me a note saying she was going back home. I think she learned that she isn't as mature as she thought. She was devastated by Jeff's arrest. Not only did she lose a job, she had her heart broken for the first time. I'm relieved. Honestly, I'm glad it didn't go any further than it did. That I know of. I'm going call later and have a talk with her." She shook her head and closed her eyes, picturing Jeff and Scheri at the festival, entwined.

"Teenagers are challenging. They aren't adults but think they are. You don't want to be too strict, but you do have to protect them. I'm not sure how well I did on that." She sighed.

Dan reached out and took her hand. "I think you did a pretty good job. She seemed like a nice enough kid and she didn't get into any serious trouble while she was here."

Tearing up, Pearl gazed into his eyes. "Thanks. I'm relieved but overwhelmed when I think of the last three months and what we all went through."

Dan patted her arm. "Speaking of teenagers, I wanted to let you know that Kaylee finally admitted that Zeus and Zora had put her up to stealing your goat. She's afraid of Zeus. Once she found out they were both in jail, she came forward. They'd told her it would be easy, promised her $50, and Zeus intimidated her by threatening to tell her parents she was smoking pot. She also admitted to being with Zeus when he stole Daisy. She's really sorry and I wouldn't be surprised if you get a written apology."

"Zeus! I knew something was wrong with that boy the first time I met him," said Pearl.

"I think there's something wrong with the whole family, not just that kid. What I want to know is, how did you figure out that Zora killed Annie? I had initially ruled her out because the hair in Annie's fist was dark and Zora has light brown hair. But you'll be happy to hear that we got the forensics from the hammer handle this morning, confirming that the only DNA on it was from Zora. We had her DNA on file because of a theft conviction about five years ago."

Pearl gloated. "When I was feeding peanuts to that ratty donkey, I noticed a piece of his mane was missing. At first I didn't put two and two together, but after everything began to point to her and her family—including the car the neighbor saw leaving the scene—I flashed back to that mane and the hair in Annie's hand. Before that, I hadn't considered that Zora might be the killer because she doesn't have dark hair. I wonder if Annie was trying to keep the donkey between her and Zora when she got hit?"

Dan shook his head, laughing. "I guess it may all come out at the trial—unless she takes a plea deal. You never cease to amaze me. Even though you sometimes drive me crazy."

"Thanks for saying that," said Pearl. "I know you're not always thrilled with me playing sleuth."

"I worry about your safety, which isn't unreasonable when you consider how a simple goat theft grew to include murder."

"Murder. I guess everyone has it in them in the right circumstances. The Vegas were in financial trouble, probably because of Tommy's gambling. I don't believe Zora went intending to kill Annie. I may not like her, but she doesn't strike me as a cold-blooded killer. I think she got more resistance than she expected, trying to cover her tracks by taking Daisy back. Still, I'm surprised. In a way, I'll miss Zora. She aggravated me no end, but I have to admit she did have a lot of goat knowledge."

"Let's hope things quiet down for a while. On another note, we still need to plan that dinner I promised you. How about next Friday night?" He raised his eyebrows.

Pearl blushed. "What time?"

"I'll pick you up at 6:00."

"It's a date," she said.

"Can you get me that milk now? I have to hit the road." He put a $10 bill on the table and stood, grinning, as Pearl got the fresh milk out of the fridge.

Dan took the milk, set it on the table and put his arms around Pearl and kissed her on the forehead. "See you then."

Did you love *Gone Goat*? Then you should read *Shed Boy*[1] by Cheryl K. Smith!

Pearl Kelly retired from nursing and moved to an idyllic farm outside of Middle Pass, Oregon, to fulfill her dream of raising miniature dairy goats. Everything is going well until her Pomeranian, Buckley, finds the body of her shed boy, Pat, while they are hiking with the goats.

The sheriff insists that it was an accident but Pearl has a feeling it was foul play. She sets out to learn who wanted Pat dead. What really happened on his last day and who had a motive to kill him. Was it jealousy? Money? Or something else?

With her helper gone, Pearl has to figure out how to keep the farm running. While learning that she's not as independent as she had

---

1. https://books2read.com/u/b5WMnA

2. https://books2read.com/u/b5WMnA

thought, she finds a way to get her goats to a show and even win some ribbons.

As Pearl investigates, she makes new friends—and at least one enemy—on the way to solving the mystery.

Read more at www.goathealthcare.com.

About the Author

Cheryl K. Smith has raised miniature dairy goats in the Coast Range of Oregon since 1998. She is an editor, freelance writer, and retired attorney. She is the author of the nonfictions books Goat Health Care, Raising Goats for Dummies, Goat Midwifery, Best of Ruminations Goat Milk and Cheese Recipes, and more. Gone Goat is the second in her Hidden Creek Farm cozy mystery series.